THE LEVIATHAN

P.K. HAWKINS

SEVEREDPRESS

THE LEVIATHAN

WWW.SEVEREDPRESS.COM

ISBN: 978-1-922861-20-7

CHAPTER ONE

Dr. Neal Markowitz stood on the deck of the research ship *Rachel Carson* and watched as the various deck hands and tech assistants did their final safety checks on the small two-person submersible that they were soon going to lower over the side and into the water. Markowitz had done hundreds of deep dives over the years, occasionally going to depths that, at that time, had previously been unheard of in human history and had given him much widespread fame. All of those dives, however, had been in vehicles that were at least still recognizable as submarines, and looking at the new, bizarre bulging rectangle of a sub that was going to be used on this one made his head hurt and his joints ache in protest with age. It was really true: they didn't make these things like they used to.

"Wishing you were still up to going down there?" someone said from behind him. Markowitz turned to see Dr. Harrison Applebaum approaching from the direction of the captain's cabin. Markowitz and Applebaum could really be father and son, everyone said, to the point it was a frequent question when either of them was interviewed. Markowitz himself didn't see it, especially since he found Applebaum's taste in facial hair styles to be highly questionable. They did both have the same short yet lanky build, and there were some facial features that had a few similarities. But while Markowitz's silvery aged hair had previously been blond, Applebaum's had a red hue that was remarkably similar to the fruit with which he shared his name. He also had a boisterous way about him that Markowitz likely would have hated in anyone else that he hadn't known as long, but the two of them had met years ago when Markowitz was spending some time teaching, and Applebaum had been his star pupil. Their relationship had become more than just professor and student some time within the last twenty years, but Markowitz couldn't for the life of him put an exact name on what it was they had.

"I could if I wanted to, you know," Markowitz said. "There's no law anywhere saying old men can't keep doing deep dives. And even if there were, we're on the open ocean. There's no one around that could possibly enforce it."

"Then do it," Applebaum said. His voice was somewhere between joking and genuine, enough that Markowitz couldn't have any guess which way it was intended. "Assist me on this one. I'd much rather have you down there with me anyway compared to who I'm going to be stuck with."

If it had been possible for Markowitz to both smile and wince at the same time, he would have. "You know I would if I could. But the sub only fits two, and you need someone who knows the technical aspects better. Trust me, Stephen Gorky is the best person for the job."

"Stephen Gorky eats nothing but burritos for lunch every day," Applebaum said. "He could be able to pilot a starship for all I care, I still don't want to be with him for hours in an enclosed space. What about Julie Morgan? Are you sure we can't switch him out for her at the last moment?"

"Morgan doesn't have as much experience as Gorky. And besides, Gorky's been promised this mission for a long time with you. You can't just switch him out at the last moment for no reason. And I've been down in the deep with worse. Gorky at least bathes on a regular basis. I knew some who didn't."

Applebaum gave a begrudging grunt, and then both stood and stared at the submersible in silence for a time. It was an NX-7 Templar model, only barely old enough to not be considered experimental. It looked like a giant, over-packed suitcase, but it had instruments on it that Markowitz had only been able to dream of in his heyday of ocean exploration. Even with some of the best research grants out there, it was unlikely they would have been able to purchase it without giant corporations footing the bill for them. That was the only thing about all this that really bothered him, although corporate sponsorship from groups like major oil companies had been pretty constant for most of his career. These companies wanted to find oil on the ocean floor, and people like Markowitz and Applebaum wanted to expand humanity's knowledge of what was down there.

Truth be told, Markowitz's discomfort with that constant arrangement was the reason he was mostly retired from the sea-adventuring life. He still loved it, but he couldn't deal with the moral conundrum any more. But Applebaum hadn't gotten to that point yet. Maybe he would one day and maybe he wouldn't. That wasn't up to Markowitz.

But he was still and always would be Applebaum's mentor and friend. And Applebaum was about to be part of the deepest dive ever known. No matter who was paying for it all, there was no way Markowitz was going to be anywhere other than by his friend's side. Or, at least, the closest thing to Applebaum's side that he could be while they were separated by millions of gallons of salt water.

"Do you ever miss it?" Applebaum finally asked after a while.

"A lot of the time, yeah," Markowitz said. "I don't know how much I would have the stomach for it anymore, though. I got the bends once or twice from coming up too fast, and it's absolutely excruciating. It feels like your entire body is on fire. And my body probably wouldn't be able to handle that anymore. It would probably kill me."

"I sense a but coming up," Applebaum said.

Markowitz smiled. "But there really is no other rush like it in the world. Going to a place on Earth no human has ever been before, seeing creatures no human eye has ever beholden in the history of our species. Or just the deep, eerie calm of having an unfathomable amount of water above, below, and all around you. Anyone who has never experienced it, they don't truly have any idea what they're missing. They may think they do. They can thought experiment with it and write about it and wax poetic, but whatever pretty words they use, they're still insufficient."

Applebaum didn't say anything. He didn't even nod. The sudden look of pure bliss on his face told Markowitz that he intimately knew exactly what his mentor was talking about.

"Boys, I trust you will be ready soon?" The voice that came from behind the two of them was deep and rough, the kind that a person would think could only come from twenty years of a two pack a day habit. But Captain James Lewis, a rugged dark-skinned man with a full beard that would have probably looked more at home on an old-school pirate, had never smoked a day in his life. He had probably earned that voice the all-natural way, by yelling at his subordinates until his vocal cords were rough and frayed. "We do have a time schedule to keep."

It always took an effort for Dr. Markowitz to not get exasperated with the captain. For one thing, he always called everyone "boys," no matter who he was talking to. Markowitz himself was roughly fifteen years older than the man, and still he would always be a boy to Lewis. For another, despite being the captain of a ship known for its deep-sea science research, he had remarkably little respect for any of the science itself. The science, in this man's eyes, was just an excuse for him to stay out on the water, and a rather annoying excuse at that. He had never been Markowitz's favorite choice to work with when he was the one leading the research, but Applebaum always insisted he be the one in charge of the actual workings of the *Rachel Carson.* And to be fair, the captain was definitely the person anyone would want in control of the ship if things ever took a turn for the worse. He was remarkably calm under any pressure at all.

"You know the safety checks aren't something that can be rushed, Captain," Markowitz said.

"I'm sorry, I thought I just heard something," Lewis said to Applebaum. "It sounded like the buzzing in my ear of a fly that doesn't actually have any authority to correct me on my own ship."

"Come on, Captain," Applebaum said. "You know anything coming from Dr. Markowitz is pretty much the same as anything coming from me."

Captain Lewis begrudgingly looked to Markowitz. "We're being told that we'll have good calm seas for the next day or so, but I just don't like the feeling of the air. I feel like the weather could turn on us at some unpredictable point, and I don't want to start seeing signs of that while your little student is buried in the waters. In my opinion, the sooner we get this dive going, the less likely it is things could go wrong."

Markowitz actually had to nod without saying anything snarky. His feelings for the captain aside, he trusted the man's judgement. Applebaum, however, would be a little different.

"You know we can't just change everything around purely because you have a feeling, Captain. Our financial backers wouldn't be happy with that. The only way we would be able to call any of this off without them reading me the riot act is if you have documented satellite data saying things could become troublesome. Do you have any of that?"

"You know I don't. But I'm also not calling for anything to be cancelled. I'm just saying that it'd personally be in all our best interests if you did your little dive sooner rather than later."

"Duly noted," Applebaum said. "Neal, if you don't mind me leaving you, I should go supervise the last of the preparations."

Applebaum left the two of them alone, but Captain Lewis apparently didn't have anything further to say to Markowitz, as he too promptly left. Feeling very much like a fifth wheel at the moment, Markowitz was just thinking about retiring to his quarters for a really quick power nap when the intern Erin Morgan nearly walked right into him.

"Whoa, Morgan. You okay?" Markowitz asked.

"Doctor, my apologies! I was just considering issues with the wind differentials and how it might affect the…"

"Morgan, maybe it's better for you to not walk and do complex engineering in your head at the same time," Markowitz said. To anyone else it might have sounded insulting for him to suggest she couldn't do the two tasks at once, but Erin Morgan was notoriously clumsy when her mind was elsewhere. It was a big reason why Markowitz didn't think she was ready to pilot the submersible, although she would definitely be great at it once she became a little more grounded and seasoned. She was only twenty, not even old enough to drink or smoke in her home state, but she was already an undergraduate with grades on her record that would terrify most people. She was fully aware that most people considered her scatterbrained, but she didn't seem to care. As long as she was allowed to be involved in missions like this, she didn't appear to mind one way or the other what anyone else thought about her.

"Sorry, Doctor. I just think that, given our current coordinates and the history involved with what we intend to find, not to mention the continued pressure of our corporate sponsor, that maybe we should… No, no, that's not it. What we really need to do is…"

Morgan seemed to completely forget that she had been in the middle of a conversation with someone and wandered off in mid-sentence, her self-lecture dropping down to a low mumble that only she could hear as she walked away.

Yes, absolutely brilliant, Markowitz thought to himself. *But definitely not ready for what might be down there.*

Later, Dr. Markowitz would remember that thought and realize that she wasn't the only one not ready for what was down there. No one was.

CHAPTER TWO

Applebaum clicked his safety harness into place and then settled into his seat. The safety harness wouldn't really be staying on him for too long. It was mostly there for when the submersible was lowered into and raised from the water, or in the event of some emergency while they were down below. Otherwise, for most of the journey down and then up again, he would have the ability to move about the tiny cabin to either look out one of the two viewports, watch the video feeds from the small outer cameras, or work the small suite of sample retrieval arms that could slide out from a small divet in the hull. Despite the small amount of time he would spend in it, though, Applebaum made damn sure to check and recheck the harness around him multiple times before he responded to the inquiries coming from the ship right outside.

"I am secure, *Rachel Carson*," Applebaum said into the small receiver next to him. "Gorky, what about you?"

"Secure as well, Doctor," he said. The man's presence wasn't offensive to Applebaum's nostrils yet, but Applebaum suspected things wouldn't stay that way, and not just because of whatever Gorky had eaten before getting into the sub. It was going to get somewhat cold down there, but whenever two people were forced into such a small proximity to each other for an extended period of time, it was sure to make the air rank before long. It was Applebaum's least favorite thing about all of this, but he had long ago decided that it was still only a small price to pay in exchange for the kind of experience that most people living on Earth could only dream of.

"Although," Gorky added, "I do wish we were still using the old two-sub protocol. No matter what the state of the modern technology is."

"Your objection is duly noted," Applebaum said as non-committedly as possible. As the ostensible leader of this particular research dive, he had to give an air of authority and assurance to everyone else involved, and that included acting like he sided with every decision made by their major corporate sponsors bankrolling the whole thing. But even on these big research missions, where companies believed they could find more resources to use for their own ends, the corporations could be cheap. Once upon a time these manned deep-sea expeditions would have two manned submersibles at once, one for the main goal of the expedition and one for support or rescue if that was needed. With a lot of modern expeditions, though, that backup wasn't needed because they were manned. Many of these were remote or robotic now. So when Applebaum had requested funding for a manned trip, the company with the wallet said that only one would be necessary. Surely, they said, these things were safe enough now that a second one wouldn't be required in the water at the same time.

And while Applebaum fully believed that this was going to be safe, that the technology in their new state-of-the-art submersible was enough for them to go against whatever the blackest parts of the sea could throw at them, he still knew enough horror stories of accidents from way back when, mostly told to him by Dr. Markowitz himself. Markowitz had even voiced some concern about the use of only one sub at a time, but he hadn't pushed back against the idea too much. Even he didn't think there was as much to worry about on these kinds of things as there had once been.

There was a lurch from outside the sub as a winch lifted it up off the deck of the *Rachel Carson* and slowly swung it over the side of the ship. Although Applebaum couldn't yet get a good look at it through the small observation ports, he knew that the shifting waters of the ocean were directly below them now, waiting to swallow the two of them up along with their tiny conveyance.

Dr. Markowitz's voice chimed in over their sound system. Although there were other people that could do this part of the job for him, Markowitz liked to be in the main control room for these missions, even when he technically wasn't any real part of the team anyway. He was mostly here as Applebaum's guest, but given his vast amount of experience with all things regarding sea exploration, no one in their right mind would tell him to get out of the control room and back to his cabin.

"Last chance check," his voice said. It was loud and clear at the moment, although that might change the deeper the sub went under the waves. There was an emergency line for the radio as part of the umbilical-like tether that would trail the sub all the way down into the depths, but even that could have a few communication problems on occasion. Mostly, though, they should be able to maintain contact just through a radio signal.

Applebaum checked the readouts again. "Everything is still hunky-dory. No problems at the moment."

"Hunky-dory?" Markowitz said over the radio. "Who the hell ever says that anymore?"

"David Bowie," Applebaum said with a smile, imagining the look of exasperation on Markowitz's face. "It was the name of one of his albums."

"Okay, first, that album was released in the seventies, and second, Bowie's dead, so I hardly think that counts as proof that people still say it."

"Well, I still say it, old man. And if you have a problem with that then…"

"We're wasting daylight, fellas," the captain said next to Markowitz. "You can mock each other some other time when we're not on a schedule."

"Party pooper," Applebaum muttered, although not without some affection. He deeply respected Captain Lewis and his abilities, but some impish part of Applebaum liked him the most simply because it was so easy to get his goat. The man really did take everything too seriously.

"Okay then, we should be ready to go," Gorky said. "Go ahead and start lowering us."

"See you on the other side," Applebaum said into the comms.

"Do you really have to say that?" Gorky asked.

"Why? What's wrong with that?"

"I know you're trying to make it sound like the other side is the other side of the expedition when we come back up, but I just can't help but think of the other side as in… you know. The other side." He made a slitting motion across his throat like he wasn't sure Applebaum would get the point without it.

"Good lord, Gorky. Relax," Applebaum said. "At this point these kinds of dives might as well be routine. You know that." Even as he said it, though, he knew that wasn't quite true. Deep dives were extremely common now, and almost always went off without a hitch. But the vast majority of such things were done with remote subs. Manned missions were increasingly uncommon. And this particular expedition would go to a depth that, personally, Applebaum had never done before. And while he was a beginner compared to old-timers like Dr. Markowitz, he was seasoned compared to almost anyone else.

But Gorky had a little experience as well, so it was unusual for him to be so squirrely about this. "Is there something wrong that you're not telling me?" Applebaum asked.

"Look, I know you're going to say it's unscientific, but I just have a feeling," Gorky said. "Something's different about this one. I woke up this morning with a sense that something wasn't completely right. I just can't put my finger on it."

"You're right. That is unscientific. Although I personally am not going to discount personal intuition as much as you would think. We'll just go slow and be hyper-vigilant about everything, okay?"

Gorky nodded. Applebaum was glad the man let it go so easily, since he didn't want to talk about it, but Applebaum himself felt more jittery than normal. He didn't think the danger was going to be anything they found down here in the depths, though. He thought back to what the captain had said about thinking the weather could turn. Maybe there was something about the pressure in the air that everyone could feel but not quite articulate.

Then again, the pressure down in the sea was always off according to human standards. It could make anyone feel like they were in some kind of oppressive environment, because they were in many senses of the word. It was always like that. Yet this one felt a little different, and Applebaum couldn't place why.

"You're in," one of the techs on the ship said over the intercom.

"Beginning the descent," Gorky said. There was a slight quaver in his voice, but otherwise he hid any trepidation he felt well.

For the next couple of hours, very little of interest happened. This particular dive was to be about four hours going down, then a half an hour at the most taking readings and gathering samples. Although this was going to technically be the deepest dive ever attempted by humans, truthfully they would only be going down about fifty feet or so more than the previous record holder. That expedition had reached the bottom of the Marianas Trench, while this one was going to be in what scans of the ocean floor detected as a slightly deeper divot within the trench. It was an expedition more for bragging rights than anything else, but there was still a good possibility of seeing something down on the ocean floor that human eyes had never seen before. The surface world may have been fully explored by this point, but down here there was always something that humankind had so far missed.

Applebaum kept a lookout through the portholes, but most of what they saw from outside came from a series of cameras in protective cases around the outside of the submersible. Everything the cameras caught, including two that were inside and pointed at Applebaum and Gorky's seats, was sent up to the *Rachel Carson* above them where it would be stored and catalogued and more thoroughly studied than they could do now in the heat of the moment. The light from the sun above the water, however, faded very quickly, and they soon had to rely on lights from the sub itself to illuminate any of the small darting sea creatures they saw for only moments before losing them. Of course, when they started to get deep enough, they didn't even need the lights as much. A number of the fish had a small glow of their own.

"Man, that will never not be freaky," Gorky said.

"What, the bioluminescence?" Applebaum asked. "It's not like the deep ocean is the only place where creatures have that. Didn't you ever catch fireflies as a kid?"

"Yeah, all the time. Especially on the Fourth of July. My family was so poor we couldn't really even afford sparklers. So that's how we lit the holiday up at night. But where I come from in Wisconsin, bugs light up while fish don't."

Applebaum didn't catch most of that. He was suddenly distracted by something he saw on one of the cameras. "Huh. Would you look at that." He pointed, and Gorky moved a little closer to see.

"Looks like an anglerfish," Gorky said. The creature on the screen was a special kind of ugly that couldn't be found anywhere near the surface. It had a large head and bulbous eyes, along with a jaw that looked akin to a steel bear trap. But the most famous and striking feature of anglerfish, no matter which variation of the species, was the long antenna that seemed to dangle over its face. At the end of the antenna a small lightbulb-like piece of flesh glowed. They used that appendage to attract the smaller glowing fish, which thought it might be another of their kind that they could mate with. When the fish got close enough, that disturbing jaw would snap closed on it.

"Yeah, but it looks like it's at least double the size of any that's been seen before," Applebaum said. "I think we're looking at a brand new…"

Something flashed across all the video monitors at once, and all of a sudden everything, both inside and outside the sub, went completely dark.

CHAPTER THREE

"Okay, will someone please explain to me what the absolute hell just happened?" The captain was looking over all the readouts in front of Markowitz, but his realm was above the water. He only had a basic knowledge of all the stuff miles below them. Markowitz was supposed to be the one who had all the answers there, and at the moment he had none.

"We've lost all contact with Applebaum and Gorky," one of Markowitz's assistants said from her place among the numerous glowing control panels.

"Everything?" Markowitz asked.

"Radio and backup communications are gone. Video is showing nothing. We're not even registering anything attached to the tether. It's like the entire sub just stopped existing."

"What are we saying here?" the captain asked. "Did it blow up or something?"

"Down there it's less likely that it would explode than it is that it would implode," Markowitz said. "But if we've lost video too, then that would include some cameras that were on the tether but not actually a part of the sub. And an implosion wouldn't have done anything to them." He stared at all the blank readings on the screen. "It's almost like… no. That can't be it. That would be impossible."

"I think I know what you're thinking, Doctor," Morgan said from nearby. She'd been so quiet for this whole time that Markowitz had completely forgotten she was even in the room, and he jumped at the sudden sound of her voice. "And while it may seem impossible, it's more likely that it's just improbable."

Markowitz stared at her. "You really think you can guess what I'm thinking?"

"Well I certainly can't," Captain Lewis said. "So is someone going to fill me in or are you two enjoying making me feel like a dumbass too much?"

Markowitz ignored him. "Okay, what is it you think I'm considering here, Erin?"

"Some kind of deep sea mega fauna."

"Wait, now that I think I understood," the captain said. He paused for a moment as the implications sank in for him. "Are you two actually suggesting that some kind of giant creature down there did something? Like what?"

"Like swallow them," Markowitz said. "Although trust me, I don't know if I believe that either."

"Something was able to sever the tether," Morgan said. "And it was able to make the submersible vanish from any of our instruments without any trace."

"Still, that doesn't exactly seem like something that would happen in the real world," the captain said.

"If you'd ever gone to the bottom of the ocean," Markowitz said, "you would have a very different idea of what is and is not part of the real world."

"Don't you both think you're making a pretty big jump to conclusions?" the captain asked. "Everything on all the monitors looked fine one moment and then in the next it was gone. There's got to be other reasons for that besides saying some monster got them."

"Maybe. Except I thought I saw something on the video feed." Markowitz turned to look at Morgan. "You must have seen it too, right? Otherwise you wouldn't be jumping to the same conclusion as I am."

Morgan nodded. "Play back the feeds. Show him."

One of the techs monitoring the equipment did as she said, and while the video was going back to the thirty seconds before everything down there had vanished, it suddenly occurred to Markowitz that he had to be in shock right now. It was the only way to explain why he wasn't a gibbering mess.

He was pretty sure that Applebaum, his student and his friend, was dead. As soon as that registered in some deeper part of him, he was sure he would break down. But for now, the analytical part of his mind set to the task of figuring out what exactly had happened.

They played the video from all the cameras, keeping the images moving slowly so they could better see what might or might not have happened. There were eight feeds in all: six pointing in all directions around the submersible, and two from inside. Although he knew that the most relevant images would be the ones from outside, Markowitz found his gaze staying on Applebaum the whole time. The two interior feeds had audio, so they could all hear the conversation happening within, although it was distorted from the slowdown.

"Huh. Would you look at that."

"Looks like an anglerfish."

"Yeah, but it looks like it's at least double the size of any that's been seen before. I think we're looking at a brand new…"

"Stop right there and just back it up a few seconds," Markowitz said. "See if you can get the fish they're seeing on the camera."

The angle of the camera wasn't quite right to view the fish in its entirety, but one camera just caught the edge of it.

"I hate to bust your theory, but I hardly doubt that thing would be big enough to swallow their sub," the captain said. "Looks like a pretty normal sized fish to me."

"Well, yes and no," Markowitz said. "It's a bit hard to make out details. That anglerfish right there, it definitely didn't do anything to them. But I don't think that's a normal-sized one, either. Size is difficult to determine in this video because there's nothing floating around nearby it that we could use as a point of reference. But I think the reason you think it's normal sized is that it's a bit farther away than you would expect. If I had to make a guess, I'd think that thing right there could be up to six or seven feet long."

"And exactly how long is an anglerfish supposed to be?" the captain asked.

"Most are under a foot long," Morgan said. "Some of the largest recorded specimens have been as long as three point three feet long, though. Which would make this one roughly twice that size."

"And at it's widest, the sub we've been using is about twenty or so feet long," the captain said.

"Twenty-one point five seven feet, to be exact," Morgan said.

"Whatever. The point I'm making is that, even if this fish we're looking at is the biggest of its kind ever recorded, it still wouldn't be enough to do what you're suggesting it did."

"You'd be right," Markowitz said. "But as I said, I don't think that particular fish is the one that did this. If that one could be two or three times the size of so-called normal anglerfish, then why not bigger? In fact, why are we making the assumption that the fish on the screen is even a full-grown adult?"

"You're suggesting that one is a baby?" the captain asked.

"I'm just trying to spitball ideas here and see what sticks," Markowitz said. He had to admit, though, that all of this seemed extremely far-fetched.

"I think you might be fixating on the wrong image," Morgan said. She pointed at a different screen. It was labeled as Camera Six, which would be the one pointing directly below the sub. "Before we backed the recording up just now, I thought I saw something on this one. Play this video back at normal speed."

The tech working the instruments looked at Dr. Markowitz as though she wasn't quite sure if she should be following the orders of a lowly intern, but Markowitz was already pretty sure that Morgan wouldn't be an intern for long. In fact, whatever else was going to be happening today,

Markowitz was starting to think she would be a key player in it all.

Markowitz nodded at the tech. “Do what she asks.”

The tech shrugged and hit a few keys on the keyboard in front of her. The video began playing, and all of them leaned a little closer to see what was about to happen.

There was darkness. Then, for the briefest moment, a pinprick of light shone deep down in the darkness.

Something happened on the screen, far too fast for any of them to immediately make sense of it, and then the feed went blank.

“Now can you go back to the same spot? But this time advance it frame by frame.”

That part turned out to be a taller order than Morgan had probably expected. In order for their research to be as accurate as possible, the expedition had spared no expense on the cameras, and they recorded at one hundred and twenty frames per second. The total length of the footage they wanted to more carefully examine was maybe seven or eight seconds long, but they didn’t dare move the footage any faster for fear of missing some important detail. The tech clicked through the initial frames at a rapid pace, but as the glow started to appear on the screen she slowed down, allowing everyone to get a much better view of the thing coming from the deep.

Despite his terror and grief at what had happened to his friend, Dr. Markowitz couldn't help but watch with his jaw dropped as the creature was slowly revealed. With each advancing frame, it became more and more obvious that this thing was some form of anglerfish, but no human eyes had ever looked at one quite like this. The light, blurry at first, resolved into a clear bulb at the end of an antenna-like appendage. Then, as the creature came up from directly below the sub, more details began to form out of the dark, each one more terrifying than the last. Its eyes were small compared to the giant, gaping maw full of sharp teeth that made up most of its face, but they bulged from their sockets like huge obsidian marbles. Although the angle was wrong for them to get a good look at its backside, they could still see the fins on either side of the fish, flapping so fast in the water that even the superior camera could not register them as much more than a blur. And between all the needle-like teeth there was a black space of nothing, framed only by a bony throat. With each advancing frame that black hole came closer until it filled the entire frame, and then nothing.

"Jesus," Captain Lewis said. "Jesus Christ on a crispy cracker. You two really were right. They're gone."

The entire room went silent. There were no words that could have possibly been sufficient to describe their dismay. And yet, for some reason Dr. Markowitz struggled to understand at first, he started to feel less despair. It wasn't that they had found an entirely new form of anglerfish that had been described before by science. Markowitz may have been a career scientist, but that kind of discovery would never have trumped the loss of a trusted friend. Instead, it slowly dawned on him that there might actually be some hope here, no matter how unlikely.

"Go back again," Markowitz finally said to the tech. "I want to try to get a better sense of the size of that thing's mouth."

"Is that really going to matter?" the captain asked. "Obviously the mouth is big enough. It crunched and destroyed the submersible."

"Yeah, that's just the thing," Markowitz said. He looked over at Morgan, expecting her own expression to start to light up as she realized what he just had, and he wasn't disappointed. "I don't think it did. Destroy the sub, that is."

"Are you in denial or am I missing something?" the captain asked. "You just saw the same footage I did. There's no way the sub survived that."

"I think maybe it did," Markowitz said. "Just perhaps not in the fashion you would normally want to think of as surviving."

"I'm lost," the captain said. "Could you please just explain it to me?"

"I think they're still alive down there," Markowitz said. "But not for long. We have to go down and get them."

"But how would we do that?" Morgan asked. "Didn't we only have the one sub?"

"There's another on board," Markowitz replied. "An old backup. It's definitely not much, but it may be their only chance." He looked over at the captain, who still seemed completely confused. "You see, it's not like anglerfish chew their prey. They open wide and swallow their prey whole. And this thing…" He pointed at the monitor showing little more than a giant's gaping throat. "Looks like it may in fact be big enough to do that to a sub.

"I think the sub may still be intact, relatively undamaged, in that monster anglerfish's stomach. But there's no telling for how long."

CHAPTER FOUR

It wasn't that Applebaum had lost consciousness. It had just felt like it, after the sub shuddered horribly and all illumination from inside and out cut off. It took him half a minute to get his bearings and realize he was still alive. But it was Gorky who spoke first.

"Why aren't the emergency lights on?" Gorky asked. "Please tell me there's nothing wrong with the power."

"The technical stuff is your area of expertise," Applebaum said. "I'm the expert on things out there, and you're supposed to be the expert on things in here." Nevertheless, he fumbled around in the darkness for where he thought the controls for such things were supposed to be. "Please tell me you did all the safety checks the right way beforehand and didn't skip anything."

"Of course I did," Gorky said. He paused before saying it again. "Of course I did." It was softer this time, like instead of trying to convince Applebaum he was trying to convince himself. “There was… there was nothing wrong. Everything passed inspection. Whatever, uh, whatever is going on, I don’t think it's necessarily a problem with the submersible.”

The eerie thing that Applebaum didn’t quite get was that it actually seemed darker inside the sub than it was outside. There seemed to be an ever-so faint blue glow coming in from the observation windows. Down this far, there shouldn’t be any light at all, and yet, unless it was some sort of trick of the mind caused by panic and sudden claustrophobia, the interior was darker than the sea itself.

Unless, Applebaum realized, that wasn’t the sea out there.

Gorky fumbled around with some controls until a small red emergency light came on above the control panels. It bathed the interior compartment in a blood-like sheen that didn’t do much for their visibility, but it was still better than nothing. Applebaum moved closer to the porthole and looked through it while Gorky looked over the instruments. He didn’t really have the context to understand what he was or wasn’t seeing, but he knew that wasn’t open water. There was something surrounding the sub, something textured, maybe something translucent. And whatever that material was, it didn’t seem to be completely black. It had a shimmery hue to it, something between blue and purple, although it was faint. It almost seemed like…

"It's bioluminescence," Applebaum whispered.

Gorky was too busy with his own tasks to hear him. He was trying the various communications options, but he wasn't having the best success. "Come in, *Rachel Carson*. Can you hear us? Dr. Markowitz? Captain Lewis? Anyone? Come on, someone up there has to be able to hear us."

"I think the tether may be severed," Applebaum said. "Any communications or systems that were relying on power from the surface won't be working."

"But those are all only the backups anyway," Gorky said. "We should still be able to get through to them. And that wouldn't explain why all our internal systems don't seem to be working." Those words seemed to send a spike of concern into Gorky, and he abandoned the communications in favor of checking other things. "Main power doesn't seem to be working, but the backups are intact. We should be able to turn some systems back on, but we'll need to be careful which ones until we have a better idea of what's happening."

"So the most essential systems only for now," Applebaum said. "And that means air. What's the status there?"

Gorky had an odd combination in his voice of calm and panicked. His voice sounded like he might break down into sobbing at any second, but his movements said otherwise. His hands shook, but that was probably from the shock more than any loss of control. Despite the jitters, his fingers effortlessly found the buttons and controls for each necessary instrument and activated or tested them as needed. "Air filtration is currently off. That's the bad news. If it stays that way for too long, we'll drown in our own carbon dioxide. The good news is I think I can get that fixed. But we're not going to be able to get out of this situation, whatever it is, unless we can get the propellors and propulsion working again, and I don't know…"

"Ignore that for now," Applebaum said. He was starting to develop a theory about where they were, a crazy one, but it was the only one that made any kind of sense with what he could currently witness outside the portholes. If it was true then it didn't much matter if they were able to make the propulsion systems work. They wouldn't actually be able to go anywhere. "Just concentrate on air. The longer it takes, the longer we breathe in our waste air, and the harder it will be for us to think straight and get us out of this mess."

We're not actually getting out of this, a small part of his mind said. *We're never leaving here. This sub is our tomb, and it's probably a tomb that itself won't even last too long*. He didn't want to think that way, but every time he glanced out the window, his hope that they might be able to survive this dwindled.

And also, it didn't look like Gorky understood yet what had happened to them. Maybe it was wrong not to tell him, but then again it might be a kindness to let the man think they had a chance for a while.

"The air purification system should have already kicked in with the emergency light," Gorky said. "Let me just…" He must have still been having trouble seeing in the red light, because he had to put his hand on some of the panels on the wall and feel his way along it before he found a small door with a clasp. "Here we go, right here. Normally I keep an emergency flashlight over here, but it must have been jostled loose and rolled away somewhere when whatever that was happened. Do you still have the one that should be over by your seat?"

Applebaum himself fumbled around for a while in the storage area next to his spot before finding a small Maglite, which he handed to Gorky. Gorky held the end of the flashlight in his teeth so he would have both hands free to work in the fuse compartment he'd found, but it was only a few seconds before the entire submersible shook slightly again, jostling the flashlight from his lips and letting it fall to the floor.

"God damn it," Gorky muttered. "What the hell is going on out there? What's causing that?" The questions, thankfully, seemed to be rhetorical and not actually requiring an answer from Applebaum. Gorky groped around on the floor for about thirty seconds before he found the flashlight again, and this time he kept the flashlight in his left hand as he went down a series of labels and switches in the fuse compartment.

"Not that one yet. Not that one. That one would… ugh, probably kill us if I flipped it in our current state…"

"Do I really want to know which of those harmless looking switches would be capable of doing that?" Applebaum asked.

"No, probably not. In fact, forget I said it. Said what? Nothing. I didn't say anything worrying at all, why do you ask?"

Applebaum couldn't be sure if he was trying to joke around or if he was actually losing it. After considering it for a few seconds, he decided that wasn't something he wanted to know either.

"Right, here it is," Gorky muttered with a sound of genuine relief in his voice. "Just got to…"

There was a loud click as he flicked a circuit breaker, and the quiet of the sub's interior suddenly filled with a gentle but insistent whirring. Applebaum took a deep breath as the air system kicked back on. It hadn't been off long enough for the air to start to taste stale, but he imagined the air tasted sweeter now anyway.

"All right. So we're not going to choke to death on our own breath," Gorky said. "Let's call that a win and move on. But before we do that, you don't happen to have any idea yet what might have happened to us, do you?"

Applebaum's eyes darted from Gorky to the porthole and then back. Hopefully it was still dark enough that Gorky hadn't seen that. "Um, I might. But I think I might want to gather more data before I say anything conclusively. Can you get any of the other instruments working?"

"Like I said, probably not on backup battery power. So I guess the next step for me is to figure out why that's all we've got at the moment."

Gorky started to take apart panels to reveal parts and wires underneath that Applebaum couldn't possibly hope to identify. It was Gorky's job to understand all the technical parts, after all, and Applebaum's job to understand everything outside the sub. So while he waited, he might as well see what he could do about confirming his theory. Not that he wanted such a theory confirmed, since he had the sneaking suspicion they were now inside something else. And as much as he would have preferred that "something else" to be a cave or wrecked ship or something to that effect, it was actually the stomach of something massive and alive.

He had no knowledge of anything that would be big enough to swallow the whole submersible, or at least not anything that would actually want to do so. And his knowledge, mostly obtained from Dr. Markowitz himself, was pretty extensive. So either that theory was way off, or they had just made a spectacular, world-changing scientific discovery in the worst way possible.

There were a couple of interesting clues outside the porthole as to what manner of creature it was that had decided to make them its meal. For one, there was the faint bioluminescence. The glow he saw didn't seem to be coming from the creature's flesh itself, or at least not the flesh of the stomach. That would mean that the light was coming from somewhere else on the creature, maybe from one concentrated spot. Secondly, the fact that he could see this light from elsewhere at all meant that the flesh was translucent. Lots of deep-sea fish had translucent flesh, since there was no need for pigment in an environment so deep sunlight never reached it. The third clue, of course, was what they had seen immediately before everything had gone wrong. One unusually sized anglerfish implied more, even though what they had seen wouldn't have been enough to attack the sub in such a spectacular manner.

With all those clues, Applebaum unknowingly came to the same conclusions about their captor at roughly the same time his mentor was doing the same on the surface.

"Found it," Gorky said. "All that jostling did something to the wires. I tell you, you wouldn't think a machine as expensive as this would have wires that could come loose so easily, but I've seen…"

Applebaum came to a quick decision. After all, there never would be a good time to share his news with his compatriot. Better to just rip the bandage right off.

"Uh, before you go too deeply into repairs, I think I have something I need to tell you," Applebaum said. The light made it difficult to see Gorky's face as he relayed all his observations, but he was pretty sure the man's look cycled through many emotions in quick succession, from annoyance to disbelief to complete terror over the course of thirty seconds.

"No," Gorky said. "There's absolutely no way."

"An hour ago I would have said the same thing. But now, there's no denying what we're seeing."

"Then how exactly do we get out?" Gorky asked. "What systems do I need to bring online to get this thing to let us go?"

"Gorky, I'm sorry. But I don't think this is something we can fix with a little ingenuity. We've been swallowed. We're quite literally fish food, and I don't think there's anything we can do other than wait to be digested."

CHAPTER FIVE

The second submersible was even drearier looking than Markowitz had feared, and yet looking at it brought back a flood of mostly pleasant memories. Unlike the one that had gone into the water earlier, this one was clearly recognizable as the type of sub he'd spent so much time in when he was younger. Once upon a time it had even been painted a bright yellow color as a cheeky reference to the famous Beatles song, but the color had faded from many hours sitting on the decks of boats waiting to be put in the water, so now it looked a little more like a sickly off-white eggshell hue. It looked decent and working in all other aspects, thankfully, but things like this had a lot of working parts. There was no telling what maintenance needed to be done on it that had been neglected over the years.

"You're really thinking of going down there in that?" the captain asked him. The two of them were standing back in the cargo hold and taking the sight in, but Morgan was right up next to it, carefully eyeing every tiny dent and scratch in it.

"We have to," Markowitz said. "It's the only other submersible we've got that can come anywhere close to being ready in a timely manner."

"Yeah. Timely. That's the real problem, isn't it?" the captain asked. "Because it took about three and a half hours for them to get down to the depth where they disappeared, didn't it? So if we really are going to try a rescue, let's say it would take about the same amount of time. Then you also need to keep in mind the prep time. Usually that would be hours."

"Except I think we can cut that time down by a lot, if we really need to," Markowitz said.

"You can cut that time down, but can you do it safely?" the captain asked.

Markowitz just looked at him with as blank of an expression as he could manage, for as long as he could manage, and eventually Captain Lewis just turned back to looking at the sub with a small shake of his head. There was no need to say it. They both knew the answer was no.

"This sub isn't rated for the same depths as the other one," Morgan said as she inspected the vehicle. Lack of experience aside, it was high time to stop having her be an unpaid intern and declare her an official part of the team and crew. She had shown by now that she knew just as much about the science and physics involved, and even the technical aspects, as many people who had actually been working with them on the *Rachel Carson* for a very long time.

“But the other one was intended to go all the way to the bottom of the Marianas Trench,” Markowitz said. “We don’t need to go down that far. We just need to go as far as they were when the anglerfish got them.”

“How do you even know that monster will still be there?” the captain asked. “It could have swallowed them and then swam away to somewhere that you’ll never find it.”

“With its belly full, it won’t even be able to go that far,” Markowitz said. Morgan flashed him a dubious look that he hoped Captain Lewis didn’t see. Markowitz could be sure of no such thing. While it seemed likely and possible, he didn’t really have any scientific basis on which to be sure. He was just guessing and telling the captain what the man wanted to hear. Because in the end, it was the captain who would decide if any of this was going to happen, and he didn’t seem entirely convinced yet. If Markowitz had to stretch the truth or tell a series of minor fibs in order to get permission to go down to try to save his friend, then that was what he would do.

“This is too risky, Markowitz,” the captain said. “I should say no.”

“We can do this,” Markowitz said.

“And who exactly is we?”

Markowitz had to pause at that one. This really was a journey that had a high likelihood of being one-way. He had no right at all to ask anyone else to come on down with him. It really was a two-person job, but it didn’t seem right in the slightest to even consider asking anyone else.

“He means him and I,” Morgan said. She said it very matter-of-factly, in a way that made Markowitz think she didn’t really comprehend how incredibly dangerous this was.

“I know exactly how dangerous this is,” she said, as though she knew exactly what his first objection would be. Markowitz was a little disappointed in himself that he was apparently that predictable. Or maybe she was just that good at reading him and others. “I’m aware there’s a high chance of this not working.”

“Then why would you volunteer for it?” Markowitz asked.

“Because this is the kind of thing I was meant to do,” she said. She ceased examining the sub to stare intently at both him and the captain. “I’ve dreamed of being an ocean explorer since I was a little girl. And I had lots of people in my family saying that it just wasn’t going to happen. Now I have the opportunity.”

“It sounds to me like you don’t truly understand the consequences if things go wrong,” Markowitz said.

"And I can't let someone who's just an intern do this kind of thing," the captain said.

That finally seemed to ruffle Morgan. "I'm always going to be just an intern if you people don't let me show you everything I can do. And Dr. Markowitz, you know I have the know-how to be your technical support."

Markowitz paused for a long time before answering. "Applebaum is my friend, and to be honest, I'm an old man. If I die trying to rescue him, that's one thing. But it would be completely another if you did."

"No, it wouldn't," Morgan said. "Just make sure the captain here knows to put my name out into the world if I don't come back. I want to be known as the person who did this with you."

Markowitz didn't like the sound of that at all. It sounded almost like she had a death wish. Then again, he really did believe that, if there was anyone at all on this ship that could go down with him and increase his chances of coming back up still breathing, it was her.

"I feel like someone has to bring this up, just so that we're all covering our asses," Captain Lewis said, "but I don't think insurance would cover her if she didn't come back. You know how crazy some of our corporate sponsors get about that kind of thing."

"You might be surprised what my family included in the personal life insurance policies they got for me," Morgan said. There was a distinct note of disdain in the way she said it which led Markowitz to believe there was a lot of bitter backstory between her and her family. She'd never talked about it before, though, and he wasn't about to pry into those sorts of things now.

"You both seem intent on throwing your lives away," the captain said. "You both know I can order you not to go down, and there would be nothing you could do about it, right?"

"You could," Markowitz said. "But is that really what you want? You would be the captain who stood by and did nothing as the lead scientist on this expedition died."

"For all I know Applebaum and Gorky are already dead. Nothing you've said so far has really convinced me that they're still alive in any way down there, or that your crazy scheme to save them has even the slightest chance in hell of working. Even if I thought there was a chance, more and more worrying weather reports are coming in. If I let you two go down, I might not just be jeopardizing you. I'd be possibly putting everyone else on this ship at risk if the weather goes bad."

"Ask around to everyone on the ship," Markowitz said. "I bet they would say that they'd be willing to risk it if there was a chance to get Applebaum and Gorky back safely." That was a bluff, pure and simple, and Markowitz sincerely hoped Captain Lewis wouldn't call him on it. There was no guarantee that every person on the crew of the *Rachel Carson* would feel that way at all. But Markowitz would try anything at this point.

The captain, however, looked like he might be coming around. "If we do this, we would have to take every safety precaution we can. I mean, the ones that we're even capable of doing in such a short period of time."

"Do you have anything particular in mind?"

"There would be another tether on this sub, but unlike the last one, it wouldn't be about keeping redundant cables or power to the sub. It would be for me to haul you back up if I decide the danger has become more than I'm willing to risk anymore. Would you be willing to agree to that?"

Markowitz actually wasn't sure that he wanted to do any such thing, but he had an idea of how he might be able to get around that if he had to. "Absolutely. Any other conditions?"

The captain paused for a long moment before responding. "If you die down there, I'll be held accountable."

Markowitz nodded. "Do you want me to leave something behind saying you should be absolved of any blame?"

"Legally I don't think that would mean anything," the captain said. "But I can't see it making anything worse. Just in case, you know?"

"I could do that," Markowitz said. "I can go write something up right now. I'm no lawyer, but I'm sure I can fake it enough to temporarily confuse any lawyers that might try to come after you. That would be about the best I could do."

"While you're doing that, I could get the sub ready," the captain said.

"I suppose I should probably write something, too," Morgan said. "You know, a message to my family in case I don't come back."

"We aren't going to have a lot of time for this," Markowitz told her.

"Don't worry. Everything I want to say to them can be written down very quickly, I assure you."

"You have about fifteen minutes or so, I would guess," the captain said. "That's probably the minimum amount of time it would take for us to get the sub up onto the deck and ready to drop in the water, but I do wish you would give us more time."

"We don't have more time," Markowitz said.

"Fine," the captain said. "But don't come over the radio and complain to me in your last moments if something goes wrong that could have been prevented with ten extra minutes of safety checks."

Markowitz laughed, although there was no actual humor in the sound. "That just reminds me that you've never been down there before. If something goes that catastrophically wrong, I don't think it likely that we'll have enough time to radio at all. We'll probably just implode."

"Yeah, well, don't do that," the captain said. "Please. I may not like you very much, but I don't really want you dead. Also, the reports I'm going to have to file about everything that's happened today are going to be long enough. I really don't want to have to write out more."

Markowitz laughed. Morgan just rolled her eyes and went to find something to write with. "We really are going to die today," she said under her breath. Markowitz caught it, but he didn't refute her words. There was an extremely high chance that she was right.

CHAPTER SIX

It took them nearly thirty minutes until they were in the water and heading down. In Markowitz's mind, that was both too short and too long of a time. Too short in that they had skipped so many of their normal precautions, and too long in that every extra minute that passed made it less likely they would find anything left of Applebaum and Gorky.

Morgan kept looking around the interior of their submersible as if she thought it would spring a leak at any moment, causing an implosion and dooming them both before they had any clue that they were already dead. Markowitz would have liked to calm her down, but truthfully, he was just as fearful of the same thing, as well as a thousand other things that he didn't think it would be prudent to mention out loud.

"You seriously used to go down in this thing all the time?" Morgan asked.

"This one? Not usually. This was just the backup module. The original is in the Museum of Science and Industry in Chicago."

"Why didn't they take this one as well?"

"Because the other one was in more displayable shape. This was the reject."

Morgan started muttering to herself. Markowitz couldn't be certain, but it sounded like she was calculating the changing probabilities the sub would implode in on them at any given second. He would have asked her not to do that, but maybe that would keep her focused. The absolute last thing either of them needed was for her mind to wander to its usual odd corners right now.

Truthfully, this old backup sub wasn't nearly as bad as everyone seemed to think, at least as far as Markowitz was concerned. He'd been down in the deep using much more cramped and much less technologically advanced models way back when he had first been starting his career. However, none of them had been able to go anywhere close to the depth they would need to reach now. And there was of course the disturbing fact that this thing had gone through only the most rudimentary safety checks before being plopped in the water. He believed it was sturdy enough to withstand the depths they needed to brave, but there was no telling what else might go wrong. The sub's hull could stay in one piece, yet it didn't really matter if something went wrong with the navigation or, may God help them, their air supply.

"This is your first deep dive, isn't it?" Markowitz asked her. He tried to keep his tone conversational and casual, but there was absolutely nothing casual and calm about anything that had happened so far today.

"You know it is," Morgan said. "They don't usually let interns do this kind of thing. Probably because we're too much of an insurance liability. Did you know that an intern has five point eight times as much of a chance of being injured on a scientific expedition as anyone else?"

Markowitz nodded, although he had no way of knowing any such thing. She could have just been throwing out random numbers to him in an effort to sound smarter, but somehow he doubted she would need to do that.

While it was ostensibly Morgan's job to take care of most of the tech issues in the sub, in actual practice, Markowitz was the one who knew the entire vehicle forwards and back. Unlike Applebaum, who really did need another person with him when he went down, Markowitz probably could have done this alone if he were younger. He just didn't have the stamina or reflexes anymore. Despite him taking care of most of the piloting work, he kept a close watch on Morgan and decided she really was capable of doing this if she had to. She really could have gone down in Gorky's place, he supposed.

They took turns doing the various tasks that needed to be done as the sub descended, but in the end there wasn't too much that even had to be done to start with. Basically, all they were doing was sinking in a controlled fashion. That left a lot of empty time, time that Morgan mostly used to mumble facts and figures to herself. Markowitz was personally fine with that, but after enough time his curiosity started to get the best of him and he couldn't help but ask her a question.

"So, I don't intend to pry…"

"Then don't," she responded without looking at him.

Well okay, he thought, and didn't say anything more. After about ten seconds, though, she sighed.

"Fine. Go ahead and ask. But let me guess what it is. You want to know what all that talk was about my family. Am I right?"

"You would be right that it's not any of my business," Markowitz said, "but you weren't exactly being subtle about some tension with your family. If I didn't know any better, I'd say you were hoping that someone would ask, because I can't help but think you really do want to talk about it."

"And what better place to talk about the tensions with my family than on a multi-hour trip down into one of the darkest places on Earth, where even if we don't die we are likely to find that people we both know have died instead?"

"When you put it like that, maybe not," Markowitz said. "But we do have a lot of time to kill, if you had something you wanted to get off your chest."

Morgan stayed silent for a very long time, long enough that Markowitz decided she really didn't want to talk at all, or maybe even that she had fallen asleep. When she did open her mouth, it was with a hushed, uncertain tone like she wasn't sure she should be saying any of this.

"I come from a very religious family," she said.

"Lots of people do," Markowitz said. "My family were very staunch and strict Catholics."

"No, I mean *very* religious. Like, borderline cult. Some people would say that I should drop the borderline part of that descriptor."

"Oh," Markowitz said. "Did you want to…"

"No, if you're going to ask if I want to say anything about which group it is or what it was like, I don't want to talk about any of that. But I wanted to get out pretty early, and I was pretty vocal about it. And my family was pretty vocal right back that if I didn't follow exactly what they did, I would not be welcome with them."

"So, more than what other people would call normal family drama, I'm assuming."

"Yeah. I got into science because, well one, I just plain had the kind of brain for it. But two, because it was about as far away as possible from what my family thought I should be doing."

"Does that mean that, when you said that everything you wanted to tell them could be written down very quickly…"

"Turns out that it took a little longer than I expected it to, but only because I found myself getting extremely creative about telling them which long sharp objects needed to be shoved up which of their various orifices."

Markowitz knew he shouldn't be amused, given that she clearly had a lot of trauma when it came to her family, but he couldn't help but laugh at that particular turn of phrase. "I hope that was cathartic."

"Maybe a little. Even if I were to die in some horrible way today, I don't think they would ever bother to read it. If someone tried to hand it to them, they would probably reject it and say that I got exactly what I deserved."

There wasn't a lot that Markowitz felt like he could say about that, so instead he simply said, "I'm sorry you've had to deal with that."

Morgan shrugged. The interior of the sub wasn't the most well-lit of places, so it was difficult to see what emotions might be crossing her face. "I'd ask you about your family, but I've already read pretty much all your books. At this point I probably know as much about you as anyone else in the world."

Markowitz tried to hide a little bit of a smile. "I don't know if I would say that. Even someone who's spent the majority of his life in the public eye has to have a few of his own secrets."

She shrugged again. After another long pause she said, "You don't really think it's possible that Applebaum and Gorky are still alive, do you? Even if they survived being ingested by a mega fauna we've never seen before, I can count at least thirty-seven different ways that they should probably have died afterward."

"Please, for the love of humanity, don't list them. I know you want to." Markowitz stared out the porthole for a while. "I just need to believe it. And I needed to act on it. You didn't have to come on down. You know as well as I do that the chances of us coming back up are not actually very good. I might have convinced the captain, but…"

"I don't think the captain was convinced at all," Morgan said. "I think he just didn't want to bother fighting with you about it. I almost got the impression that he wouldn't have given you any resistance at all if it weren't for me being with you."

"Which, again, makes me wonder why you were so adamant on it," Markowitz said.

"Because I just need to. Just, you know, deep within my bones. Maybe that's not something you can understand."

Markowitz thought back to all his ocean adventures of years past, of all the dangers he'd endured just so that he could be the first to see or do something that no one else had ever done before. "No, I actually think it is."

Morgan toggled between several of the cameras on the outside of the sub, quickly going through the various images around the sub. There were four in total on this one, unlike on the submersible that Applebaum had gone down in, and the picture quality wasn't at the same level. While Markowitz had made sure early in the dive that all four were working, he couldn't help but notice that one now only showed a blank screen. That could be because something in the camera itself just wasn't working right, or it could mean that they were starting to get to depths where some of the equipment on the outside couldn't take the pressure anymore. That was worrying, and he would have mentioned it to Morgan, but he realized that it was unlikely she hadn't already figured that out for herself.

"Are all of these cameras recording?" she asked.

"They should be, but we didn't have the time to set them up to beam the images back to the *Rachel Carson*. Any recordings made by us here are going to share whatever fate we do."

She didn't respond to that. She just kept going through the images.

“We should be approaching a similar depth to where they were when they disappeared,” Markowitz said. “You keep looking at the cameras and I’ll keep an eye out through the portholes.”

There were definitely things to see down here, many small creatures and a few bioluminescent fish, but for a few minutes there was nothing that indicated any anglerfish. Soon, however, she stopped flipping through the images and pointed at the monitor. “There. I think I see something that might be similar to that first mystery anglerfish we saw on the video.”

“Do you think you can maneuver the sub so that we can look at it through the window?”

“Why not just watch it on the monitor?” Morgan asked, but before he could answer she came to his reasoning herself. “Because we should try to keep the monitor on a camera pointed in a downward direction just in case the thing that got Gorky and Applebaum comes back. Right. Got it.”

But as she turned the sub, it became obvious that they wouldn’t have to watch the monitor for what had gotten the other sub.

The creature was already out there.

CHAPTER SEVEN

It was crowded with both of them pushed so tightly together to see out one window, but neither of them paid too much attention to the other. It was impossible to pay attention to anything other than the massive beast outside.

Thankfully, it wasn't directly outside. There still seemed to be quite some distance between them and it, which contributed some difficulty in terms of putting the proper context to its size, just like the first of these anglerfish that they had seen on screen back when they were still above the water. This time, however, this particular fish had a new detail that helped them. It had a bulging belly in the vague shape of the other submersible. And honestly, the sub inside it wasn't making the bulge that large. Based on that info, Markowitz had to guess that the creature may have been up to forty or fifty feet long.

"I had no idea it was going to be that big," Morgan muttered.

"It swallowed an entire two person sub," Markowitz responded. "How on earth would you not think it would be gigantic?"

"I mean, I knew it was going to be huge, but this is just…" She waved her hand wildly at the window as if that was sufficient to end her sentence for her. And honestly, it was. Mere words were insufficient to describe this thing. This wasn't just large for an anglerfish. This thing was large for anything currently living in the modern ocean except maybe for a blue whale. And to be honest, they had no way of knowing if this thing was even grown to its full size, so there was always the chance that a blue whale might be a tad smaller.

And, Markowitz suddenly realized, they were shining their lights directly at it, giving it the perfect way to track them.

"Shut off all the exterior lights," Markowitz said. "The rest of the interior ones, too, everything that isn't essential. We don't want it thinking we're some kind of large exotic bioluminescent fish."

"Which is probably exactly what it thought the other sub was," Morgan said quietly.

Markowitz nodded but declined to add any more commentary. There was nothing useful he could add that wouldn't scare the pants off of her and, truth be told, of him.

In many ways it did seem just like the anglerfish he'd known of previously. It had the antenna and the protruding jaw along with similar freakish eyes, but the shape of its fins were different than others, and they were larger, as well. This was a creature that likely could swim much faster than its smaller brethren. That was probably how it had come up from under Applebaum's sub so quickly without them realizing they were being hunted.

"It's amazing," Morgan said quietly. "If this were some bad Hollywood movie, the reason this thing exists would be because of genetic experimentation by a mad scientist or something. Or a toxic waste spill or something stupid like that. But that's not what's going on here, not for real. This really is just probably the product of millions of years of evolution, and yet we have somehow managed to never see anything like this yet."

Markowitz nodded, continuing to look at the various images of the thing on the monitors with awe. "It's easy for us to forget how small and insignificant we really are. I guess every once in a while nature needs to find a way to remind us."

"Should… should we try to get closer to it?" Morgan asked.

Under any other circumstances at all, Markowitz's answer would have been a resounding "No way in Hell." But they hadn't come down all this way just to run screaming from the enormous creature they had already hypothesized was down here.

“We should,” Markowitz answered, “but we should report in to the *Rachel Carson* first. Just…” He caught himself from saying anything further, but Morgan was on the same page and filled in the rest of his sentence for him.

“Just in case we end up exactly like Applebaum and Gorky,” she said.

He nodded. Probably he was the one who should make contact with Captain Lewis over the radio, but the mention of his maybe-alive-maybe-deceased friend distracted him. He was suddenly overcome with an urge to recklessly steer the sub directly toward the fish while letting out an absurd war cry, but that would hardly do anything worthwhile.

While he kept staring, Morgan took the radio. “Come in, *Rachel Carson*. Do you read us?” She stopped for a second, looked quizzically at the equipment, and then added, “over?”

“You don’t need to say ‘over,’ Miss Morgan,” Captain Lewis replied back. “This isn’t the seventies and we’re not long-haul truckers.”

“Um, okay,” Morgan said. “We’ve located the creature that swallowed Applebaum and Gorky.”

“Now please tell me you’ve spent the trip down there coming up with a better plan than ‘Let’s get closer and see what happens,’” the captain said.

Markowitz got closer to her so he could speak to the captain as well. "You're pretty much asking us to lie to you. We can't really assess the situation very well from this distance. Honestly, we're only doing this as a courtesy call in the event that something happens."

The captain was quiet for a time before answering. "Fine then. But from this point on keep in constant contact with us. If more than thirty seconds goes by without me hearing so much as breathing from you two, I'm pulling an emergency abort on this whole thing. Got it?"

"Roger," Markowitz said, then smiled. "Over."

The captain's sigh over the radio was audible and exaggerated.

"Alright," Markowitz said to Morgan. "Take us closer, slowly. Keep off all lights that we don't absolutely need. And keep toggling through the video feeds looking for anything, well, you know, fishy."

"Why would there be anything else out of the ordinary?" Morgan asked. Markowitz didn't answer, since he was sure she would come up with plenty of answers for that herself. "Oh," she said. "Okay. Proceeding with caution."

"And move as slowly as is possible," Markowitz said. "The last thing we need is for it to sense our motion in the water and get spooked. If it decides to swim away, we may never find it again. We're unbelievably lucky as it is that it decided to stay in roughly the same place as where it had its meal."

Even using the bare minimum lights down here in this deep, dark nothingness, they could see just enough to confirm many of the conjectures they'd made about the creature from the brief video they had seen above. It was very clearly in the same family as "normal" anglerfish, but there were enough differences, other than the obvious one of its size, to identify this as something new to science. Even with its superficial resemblance to it smaller cousins, this thing could in fact be a brand-new species altogether, for all Dr. Markowitz knew. He wouldn't be able to say much for certain without being able to study a sample, whether in the wild here or in a lab, but they didn't have the luxury of time for that. There was already a very good chance that the two men who had been swallowed by this thing were dead, and if they weren't then it seemed unlikely that they would have much time left.

"While I understand your reasoning," Morgan said, "I really think we're going to need to turn on a light at some point. If we're going to come up with a plan, then we'll need to know details that just aren't going to be visible to us."

"You may be right. Cut all the propulsion for a moment, but keep it ready to be turned back on at a moment's notice for a quick escape if we need it.

Let's see how close we can get to it just by drifting."

The anglerfish didn't seem to be actively moving in the water. It was just floating aimlessly, almost like it was asleep, even though that was something few fish actually did. It did at least seem to be in some low-energy restful state, at least, likely a result of having recently consumed such a large meal. Hell, for all they knew it could even be dead, for all they understood about this creature. But the bulb hanging in front of its face still glowed an eerie blue, and Markowitz suspected that inner light would fade if it were no longer living.

"So here we are, sitting right in front of a fish that could probably swallow the one that swallowed Jonah," Morgan said. "What exactly are we going to do now?"

"I guess the first order of business is to determine if our friends are still alive inside, and if they are, we need to figure out a way to communicate with them."

"What about the radio communications?" Morgan asked. "They might be cut off from the *Rachel Carson*, but from this distance maybe we'll be able to communicate with them ourselves. The only thing between them and us now is a little water and some fish skin."

"That's as good of a place to start as any," Markowitz said. He had her do a quick report in to

Captain Lewis letting him know that they were going to need to switch channels for a moment, then made her dial in to the frequency that the other submersible had been on.

"Applebaum? Gorky? Do you read?" she asked, then mischievously added, "Over."

They waited for several seconds, but nothing came back. She repeated it two more times, this time leaving out the "over," but at no point was there an answer.

"That doesn't mean anything," Morgan said in a voice that somehow managed to sound hopeful and despondent at the same time.

"No, it doesn't," Markowitz said, even though he wasn't quite sure if he believed it. "They've been inside that thing for hours. It would make sense that some parts of it have been damaged by digestive juices. That doesn't mean the integrity of the sub has been compromised yet." Markowitz wasn't exactly sure where in that particular model of submersible the communications equipment would be. It was so new he couldn't even be sure what *kind* of equipment it had. A professor on a deserted island could have made its comms system out of a pair of coconuts and he still wouldn't be aware.

"So what's the next option, then?" Morgan asked. "If we can't talk with them through radio, then what else even is there? Going up to the fish and poking it in its belly?"

Markowitz thought about it for a second, then shrugged. "Yeah. I suppose that probably is the next attempt."

"I was joking," Morgan said. "Please say you are, too."

"I don't think I am. Our options are extremely limited right now. We could flash our lights in some variation of Morse Code, but we have no way of knowing if they'd be able to see through the skin enough. It would also attract unwanted attention from the fish."

"And going up to it and jabbing it in the belly like it's the Pillsbury Doughboy won't?"

"Honestly, I don't even know. If you have a different, better idea, then I am absolutely ready to listen to it."

Morgan thought for a few seconds, then shook her head. "I'm embarrassed that I don't have one."

"Then power up the propulsion. We're going to move gently."

Morgan did as she was told, and the sub inched closer to the huge creature. The thing was large enough that it didn't seem to know or care that they were there. At the moment it didn't perceive them as a threat. As long as they could also keep it from perceiving them as food, they should be okay.

"Alright, hold on for contact," Morgan said. "We should be bumping it in three… two… one."

The sub shuddered slightly as it pressed against the outline of the sub in the anglerfish's stomach. The fish twitched a little, like it didn't like that but didn't think of it as much more than an annoyance, either. Otherwise, it did nothing.

Nothing that they could see at least.

They would learn soon enough, though, that the anglerfish might be able to do things they hadn't thought of yet.

CHAPTER EIGHT

Applebaum roused from a drowsy restlessness as something outside the sub caused the entire thing to shudder. At first, he thought it had to be the digestive fluids of the anglerfish's stomach finally eating away at the outer hull enough to rupture it, and that their death was imminent. But after a few seconds of not imploding, he looked around to see that, so far at least, the sub seemed fine. It was designed to resist levels of pressure beyond anything any other sub had ever experienced before, after all, so maybe it would keep its integrity for a long time. Possibly even long after its two occupants had died of starvation or dehydration.

Yeah, Applebaum thought, that's a cheery idea.

Gorky had passed out too, but he was a little slower to wake than Applebaum. That probably wasn't a good sign. The carbon dioxide levels in the sub were probably keeping him sleepy. It would also affect their reflexes if they found themselves having to act quick on something.

I really do think we're not going to be getting out of this, Applebaum thought. Just as he thought that, though, there was another shake from outside the sub. It didn't just seem to be the interior of the stomach that was rumbling. Something seemed to be disturbing the anglerfish from the outside.

"Now what the hell could be causing something of this size problems?" Applebaum muttered to himself. He looked out the porthole again, not expecting to be able to see much more than the skin of its belly still stretched over their vehicle, but he was wrong. The translucent belly made it possible to see just a little outside of the fish, but not enough to make out any positive details. He could definitely see, though, that there was something relatively nearby that was of a larger size. Not anywhere near as large as the creature that had swallowed them, but it was still much bigger than most fish or sea creatures that should have been down here.

"You know, if I didn't know any better, I would say…" Applebaum trailed off as an absolutely nutty idea occurred to him. "No way. He wouldn't."

"Who wouldn't do what now?" Gorky mumbled. He too had fallen asleep, as there was little else either of them was able to do beyond waiting for death to take them. They had tried to talk to each other in the first hour or so in an attempt to keep things light. There had even been idle talk of a possible rescue. But in the end both of them had known that no such thing was feasible. While neither of them had discussed it yet, Applebaum was sure that, before much longer, talk would come back, and it would be about what they would need to do to ensure that their long, painful deaths were shorter and more merciful. Already the interior of the sub smelled with the unfortunate indignity both of them had been forced to endure after being stuck down here longer than expected with no bathroom of any sort, and as such embarrassing moments piled up, it wouldn't be long before Gorky started to think in the same direction as Applebaum, if he hadn't already begun to do so.

Except, now, Applebaum started to wonder if the impossible idea of getting out of this was actually just merely improbable. "There's something else outside the fish," Applebaum said.

Gorky yawned. They were both yawning a lot at this point, and Applebaum at least was starting to feel a dull headache. Both were signs that the air was not providing them with quite the amount of oxygen they needed. "Yeah," Gorky said. "It's called water. I've heard a rumor that there's a lot of it out there somewhere."

"No, listen, don't be snarky," Applebaum said. "I'm serious. I think..." He almost didn't want to say it for fear of getting his own hopes up, and yet at the same time he desperately wanted it to be true. "I think maybe Dr. Markowitz and Captain Lewis might be trying to mount some kind of rescue."

Gorky sat up a little straighter in his seat, although he still seemed groggy. "That's not possible, is it? How would that even be possible?"

Applebaum tried to concentrate on what his mentor would be thinking. It was difficult. Not only was there the questionable quality of their air and the contaminated environment they were in, but he was also having trouble concentrating due to hunger. If everything had gone correctly, he would be back up on the *Rachel Carson* now with a bellyful of whatever they were throwing together in the mess today. He thought tater tots might have been on the menu. He struggled to keep his mind on their current situation while it was filled with the thought of potatoey and ketchupy goodness.

"There, um, there was another submersible that was still on the ship as a backup," Applebaum said. "But it's never been tested at these depths. Trying to use it would be extremely dangerous."

"So dangerous that Markowitz wouldn't try it?" Gorky asked.

"No," Applebaum responded. "I'm not sure if there is such a thing, if he were that obsessed or determined."

"And would we be something he would be that determined to retrieve?"

Probably not you, Applebaum thought. *Just me*. Even though he knew he shouldn't say that, in his punchiness he felt the words start to bubble up to his mouth, and it took a concentrated effort to keep his lips from opening and spilling out something mean. But it wasn't really mean. It was simply the truth. Dr. Markowitz might not come down in a rickety old sub for just anyone. But for his prized pupil? That was a distinct possibility.

"Yes," Applebaum finally said. "But I don't know if…" There was another small shudder around the sub, followed by a sound like the hull creaking under pressure. While the anglerfish's stomach might not have evolved to dissolve plastic, three or so hours of attempted digestion were probably enough to start making the outer portion of the sub lose some of its integrity. If they had been at even lower depths than where they currently were, it might have been enough for the sub to finally collapse in upon itself under the pressure. It seemed unlikely that it would still be capable of keeping them alive in here after another couple hours of this.

Which is why it was good that the initial shudder had again felt like something prodding them from outside the fish.

"While I would love to believe you that they somehow mounted a rescue," Gorky said, "I think it's far more likely that we're soon going to run out of time."

"Actually, I think it might be both," Applebaum said. "Try the radio. See if anyone is trying to get through to us."

It was evident very quickly that, even if someone was, they wouldn't be able to hear it. The sounds that came through the receiver were sickly and unidentifiable. The radio wasn't going to be much help to them.

"If there is someone out there…" Applebaum began.

"And that's a really big if," Gorky interrupted.

Applebaum began again. "If there is someone out there, we need to find a way to communicate with them." He sat for nearly thirty full seconds before his punch-drunk brain came up with the most obvious answer. "Morse code."

"We've already established there's no way for them to hear anything we send them," Gorky said, "so how would that possibly work?"

"We don't use sound. We use sight," Applebaum said. "I know we gave up on that earlier, but see what you can do about getting some of the exterior lights on."

"Again, what good is that going to do?" Gorky asked. "We are inside a fish, in case you didn't remember."

"A fish that has no good reason for pigmented skin. A fish that, in many of its smaller brethren, can be seen through. Parts of it may glow, but not anything in its belly. If they see a light coming from here, even a faint one, we'll be able to use it to signal them."

"What the hell. Why not try," Gorky muttered. "I certainly don't have anything better to do with the last hours of my life." They hadn't tried to do much with the exterior lights earlier, since what would be the point, but as Gorky set to work seeing what they were still capable of, they discovered that roughly half the exterior lights were gone, either broken by their trip down this thing's gullet, or damaged by the digestive fluids. Half, however, was still a lot better than none, and Gorky was quickly able to get enough working that he could use to rapidly switch on and off.

"So you're going to have to help me with this," Gorky said. "Morse code isn't exactly something I ever made a priority to learn."

Applebaum would have chided him for that, but Gorky wasn't the only one who had slacked off when it came to that sort of knowledge. "Dr. Markowitz doesn't really know it either."

"Uh, if he doesn't know then how…"

"I know he at least knows SOS. The two of us have had occasion to use that much before." He had Gorky flicker the lights in a pattern of short-short-short, long-long-long, short-short-short. Then they both waited to see if there was any kind of sign of life from outside the fish.

There was a very long pause, enough that Gorky asked if they should do it again and Applebaum started to think he'd just been experiencing wishful thinking. Then there was finally a flash from outside, a diffused and difficult to see light that nonetheless could only have been from another sub.

Both Applebaum and Gorky tried to cheer, but their throats were too raw and hoarse from lack of hydration for them to do much.

"I'll be damned," Gorky said. "They're actually out there. I can't believe they actually did that."

Applebaum wanted to say that he could, but he didn't want to speak up just yet. Just because there was another living human somewhere nearby didn't mean they all weren't still in extreme danger.

Another light flashed from outside. This one was on for longer, and even more faint than the first.

"What the hell?" Gorky asked. "There's more than one sub out there? Never mind getting one extra sub down here. Doing it with two is… I don't like using this word lightly, but it's miraculous."

Yes, it really is, Applebaum thought. Except the problem was that he didn't believe in miracles at all.

Another faint glow came from somewhere out there. This one stayed on for much longer, and moved some distance before it went out again.

Applebaum felt the blood start to drain out of his face as his sleepy brain started to put together an idea of what was going on.

"Something is wrong," Applebaum said. "Something is very long, uh…" His speech was starting to mess up. If they were going to survive long enough to possibly be rescued, which suddenly felt much less likely than it had only a minute earlier, Gorky was going to need to take a look at the air filters very soon. "I mean, something is very wrong."

"I don't…" Gorky started to say, but he trailed off as another blob of light speedily approached and then darted away. Only now did Applebaum realized that most of the lights they were seeing were different from the first one. That one had had a yellowish tint to it, while these others seemed to be more bluish.

"Those are not other subs out there with them," Applebaum said. "Those are more anglerfish. And not the small normal kind."

CHAPTER NINE

Markowitz couldn't pinpoint the exact moment he realized the monster anglerfish wasn't alone. The others didn't dramatically announce their presence the way the first one did, swimming up from the deep and attacking them with jaws wide open. Instead, many faint glows could gradually be seen out in the blackness, darting in and out of view and back and forth. As they got brighter and clearer it became impossible to try dismissing them as the smaller varieties.

Both Markowitz and Morgan stared as one enormous fish became two, then three, then four. At the moment, none of them seemed particularly inclined to attack their sub. Probably that was because they had most of their exterior lights out and as many of the interior ones as they could and still be able to work. They'd flashed the exteriors at the front of the sub briefly for the benefit of the two people trapped inside the first fish, and maybe that was what had attracted the rest of these. But as long as their sub was still and mostly dark, nothing more was happening.

"Dr. Markowitz? Miss Morgan?" the captain asked over the radio. "You've been quiet for too long. Respond or I'm going to assume we're in an emergency situation."

"I don't know if I would call it an emergency yet," Markowitz responded, "but we've certainly found something concerning. Do you want the good news we have or the bad news?"

"Markowitz, quit dicking around and just say what you need to say."

"Fine, Captain. We now know for a fact that Applebaum and Gorky are still alive inside the first anglerfish. That's the good. The bad is that there's more of them."

"What do you mean, there's more of them?" the captain yelled over the radio. Markowitz could just imagine his shocked face as he screamed, complete with that vein in his forehead that always popped out when he heard bad news.

"What do you mean, what do I mean?" Markowitz asked back. "I thought I was pretty clear. There's more than one anglerfish."

"Please for the love of all that's holy tell me that the rest of them are normal sized."

"If they were normal sized it wouldn't exactly be something I felt the need to report, would it?"

There was a long pause from the other end of the radio. "Exactly how many are we talking here?" The captain suddenly sounded a lot calmer, which honestly Markowitz didn't take to be a good sign. An entire school of monster-sized anglerfish wasn't the kind of thing that would inspire calmness in anyone who truly understood the situation down here.

"Six or seven," Markowitz said. It was difficult to be certain in the black depths, even with their bioluminescent lights. "Or at least that many females. Technically there could be males as well with them, for all I know."

"Why are you not acting like that would be so much worse?" the captain asked.

"Well, you see, because of the sexual dimorphism seen in any other anglerfish, the males would actually be…"

"You know what? Never mind," the captain said. "I don't actually want to know anything about anglerfish sex. But six or seven of the females, you're pretty sure about that?"

"Pretty sure." Markowitz stared out the porthole and watched intently as the school of anglerfish swam about. Despite the very similar anatomy of these fish to the typical kind that had previously been known to science, this behavior of swimming in a school was not something that he had ever actually observed in the smaller species. Anglerfish were already enigmas, their habits hard to observe in the wild due to the extreme depths at which they lived, but after just seeing this group of them like this, Markowitz had to admit that he couldn't make any assumptions at all as far as predicting how these monsters of the deep might act. Even the most basic scientific facts he was supposed to know about their biology could very well be wrong. Every single thing he or anyone else thought they might know about these monsters of the deep had to be taken with a grain of salt.

There was a jolt from the top of the sub, and the view outside their window shuddered. The swirling school of giant fish, still not paying much attention to them yet, appeared to drop slightly. No, Markowitz realized. The fish weren't dropping. The sub was going up.

"What the hell?" Markowitz yelled over the radio. "Lewis, are you pulling us back up?"

"I am," Captain Lewis said. "I'm aborting this whole thing. I should have cut it all off earlier. Way earlier. I'm done playing around."

Markowitz made sure to shut off their end of the communications before he said anything in return. "Then I guess it's good for us that I'm not playing around either."

"Cheesy and cliché, but intriguing," Morgan said. "And just what exactly do you mean?"

"I mean I thought it was a possibility he would do this, so I made sure to set something up." Markowitz fiddled around near his seat, looking for something he had left there immediately after he'd gotten into the sub. "The one good thing about the near complete lack of safety checks on this trip is that no one got a chance to notice a rather obvious bit of sabotage that I myself did to the sub right before we got in."

"Okay, now we're going from intriguing to alarming," Morgan said.

"They're not really used anymore, but during some of my early sea adventures we had some troubles where we would need some small, uh, explosives."

"Yeah, still alarming. You're not inspiring confidence here."

"Look, just… I hid the remote for it under my seat." Given the cramped quarters, it was actually harder to reach under his seat than he had thought it would be, and every moment he spent fumbling around for his hidden contraband was another moment that they were being pulled further away from their in-danger friends. Also, from the way the multiple giant anglerfish had started swimming around faster, it seemed like their sudden movement was agitating them. And the last thing he wanted was for things of that size to feel annoyed or threatened. "Can you get on the radio and try to stall the captain while I get it?"

"How would I…" Morgan started, then stopped as she had a thought. "I've got an idea." She turned the radio on and spoke into it with a disconcertingly conversational tone. "Hi Captain

Lewis. This is Erin Morgan. How are you doing today?"

"Miss Morgan, I don't know what you're trying to…"

"Captain, do you ever go fishing?"

"Uh…"

"You know how when there's a fish in the water and you've got the bait sitting on the hook and the fish isn't doing much so you waggle the fishing rod or reel the hook in just a little to get the fish's attention and all of a sudden the fish snaps at the bait and you're suddenly pulling the fish in instead of just the bait?"

"Um, yes, but…"

"*Well you're doing that right now! Stop pulling us in or we're going to be the bait!*" she screamed. A few seconds later, the sub stopped going up by itself.

"Good job," Markowitz said as he finally found the remote.

"It helps that everything I said is pretty much true, but it probably won't stop him for long," Morgan said. "I'm betting he's going to resume pulling us back up soon, just slower. So whatever you're going to do, you better do it now."

Markowitz finally got the remote out and showed it to her, then proceeded to turn it on and arm it.

"I really hesitate to ask exactly how this is going to work," Morgan asked.

"The explosive charge is small, so it's not like we need to worry about it doing any additional damage to the sub. It's specifically designed to sever only the cable that it's attached to. We've had to use it in the past to sever knots and tangles in ropes or cables that were putting us in danger," Markowitz said. "Although this time I suppose we're expressly using it as a way to keep us *in* danger."

He hesitated for just a second. Captain Lewis was likely very right in trying to haul them back up. The likelihood of any of this being survivable if they stayed down here was small, as was the likelihood of being able to free another submersible from inside the gut of one of the biggest fish humanity had ever seen. If he pressed this button, probability stated he and Morgan would never go back up.

But he had to try for Applebaum's sake. He was pretty sure the other man would do the same for him. They had done too much together to just give up when he was already this close. However, it wasn't just him and Applebaum and Gorky who could die here.

"Erin, before I do this, I need to…"

"Yeah, yeah, yeah. I know. Cover all your bases, make sure I understand the risks and how we probably won't survive, I'm young and have so much to live for. Whatever. Just skip the speech, assume I give my approval, and press the damned button already while you still can."

Markowitz almost smiled, but held himself back. With a shrug, he pressed the button.

Morgan looked like she was expecting some kind of big shudder, but all either of them felt was a slight thump from above. It was a light enough sound that, if Markowitz hadn't known in advance what it was, he would have thought it was them bumping into a small fish or something.

"Wait, that's it?" Morgan asked, then did a passable expression of Marvin the Martian. "I was expecting an earth-shattering kaboom."

"That's it for us," Markowitz said, "But if you want an explosion of some kind, I suggest you keep the radio on and wait about three or four seconds."

He counted silently in his head. He was wrong. It took six seconds before Captain Lewis's voice screamed over the radio.

"God damn it, Markowitz, what the hell did you just do?"

Now Markowitz really did smile as he replied. "Why, Captain, I'm sure I have absolutely no idea what you mean."

"You know full well what I mean. We're trying to pull you back up and have completely lost all tension. Which means your sub is no longer attached. So help me God, if…"

Markowitz interrupted. "Four hours, Captain. If one or both of the subs aren't back on the sub in four hours, then you will know that all of us down here are dead. But at least give us that much. Because I really believe we can pull this off."

He didn't wait for the captain to cuss at him in return. He simply switched off the radio, right along with any other way that the *Rachel Carson* might be able to contact them. It wasn't in any way the smart thing to do, but then again, they had stopped caring about the smart thing to do the instant they had decided to try a rescue mission.

"Give it to me straight," Morgan asked. "Were you lying just now?"

"Which part?" Markowitz asked.

"The part where you said you really believe we can pull this off. Was that true?"

Markowitz considered lying to her as well, then realized that wouldn't do either of them any good. "Oh hell no. You probably know the odds far, far better than I do. I'm actually fairly certain I've just doomed us to a watery grave."

Morgan nodded. There was some fear in her face, but not nearly as much as there probably would have been in anyone else. "Good to know. Now let's get to work proving us both wrong."

CHAPTER TEN

Applebaum knew that something was going on outside the anglerfish, something involving the other sub, but he couldn't for the life of him figure out what that was. The fish's belly may have been translucent, but when there was little to no light out there, the best he could see was a series of vague impressions involving a number of things moving. Most of them were larger but possibly more distant; he could only assume those were other anglerfish very similar to the one they were inside right now. Occasionally he could see small glows from them. But the flashing lights from the sub didn't happen again for a long time, and he had no way of knowing if that meant they were in danger or trying something to help them.

While he spent all his time intently staring out the porthole trying to understand, Gorky was over in his area fiddling with various bits of electronics. Something he had done had made the air seem less stale, thankfully, and consequently neither was feeling quite so loopy as they had earlier. It was amazing what a little hope could do for someone's ingenuity. But even if it was easier for them to breathe, they still had to operate on the assumption that they had a time limit. Deep sea stomach acids might not have been the best against the hardened plastics and polymer alloys that made up the sub, but eventually they would erode the integrity of the sub enough for it to break apart under the pressure. They had to have some ideas of what to do long before then.

"We need to put our heads together about how to get out of this," Applebaum said.

"We've been trying to think of things for hours," Gorky said. "It's not like anything has changed."

"Of course something has changed," Applebaum said. "We no longer have to do this alone. We've got help."

"Alright then. Start brainstorming. How exactly does one get out of the belly of a giant anglerfish?"

"I don't know," Applebaum said with a shrug, but even as he said that, he wondered if maybe they were overthinking it. "Maybe it's just the simple matter of going really fast and busting out."

"What, you're expecting us to ram our way out of this thing's stomach?" Gorky asked. "I hate to break it to you, but this submersible is very clearly not going to be capable of something like that."

"On our own, probably not," Applebaum said. "But if they're doing something out there at the exact same time, maybe there's a chance."

"But that would require a level of coordination we're just not going to get," Gorky said.

"Maybe, maybe not," Applebaum said. "We need to get the cameras working again and feeding images in to us. Any idea if we can make that happen?"

"Hell, I don't know," Gorky said. Then he seemed to pause and really think about it. "I don't think I could get all of them to work. We're on emergency power, remember. But one or maybe two if we're lucky, that I might be able to make work. Would that be enough for whatever crazy shit you're thinking?"

Applebaum paused before nodding. "I think so, but it would have to be the camera most directly facing the anglerfish's front. As in, its throat and mouth."

"Right. I see," Gorky said. "When this thing opens its mouth, we want to be able to see and make a break for it. The problem is, how do we get it to open wide? It's not like it's going to try to eat something else, is it? I would think that it's going to be pretty satisfied with a huge meal like us for quite some time."

Applebaum nodded, although honestly he couldn't be completely sure. Anglerfish weren't his most direct area of expertise, so he wasn't completely sure how long the digestion process was for them. And even if he did know, he couldn't make any assumptions that it would be the same for this one. There was also the fact that this giant was probably more used to eating standard fish, not subs made of experimental composites. It would take a lot longer for this thing to be finished with them. Of course, that might actually work in their favor, as well.

"Think about it from the fish's perspective," Applebaum said.

"Uh, not a perspective I would often say I consider."

"It might have thought we were some kind of exotic prey when it was swallowing us, but we're still sitting in its stomach hours later with, I hope, only minor damage from its stomach acids."

Gorky started to nod, and there was an actual glimmer of hope and excitement in his eyes. "Indigestion. It probably feels like it needs the world's biggest Alka-Seltzer right now."

"So getting it to open its mouth to spit us back up might not be so far fetched at the moment," Applebaum said.

"Okay. Then what do we need to do to give it that final push to vomit us up?" Gorky asked.

"We'll need to do something from inside here to give it even more of a bellyache than it already has."

"Well, we can try to move the submersible around as much as possible. You know, really make it feel us. But I don't know if that alone will be enough. Hopefully Dr. Markowitz or whoever else is in that other sub will also try to poke it from the outside. Some large predators in nature that swallow their prey whole, they will vomit it back up if they're in danger. Right? At least, I thought I heard of that being a thing."

Applebaum nodded. "Snakes have been known to do that, although an anglerfish is a long way from being a snake. That shouldn't matter, though, as long as they do something out there to threaten it at the same time we make our attempt to get out. It shouldn't know what hit it either way."

"But that's still going to require some kind of coordination with them outside the fish," Gorky said. "And faintly seeing flashing lights isn't the best way to communicate."

"Hmm," Applebaum said. "Maybe not normally. But if… wait…" He looked back outside to see if he could again see any sign that the other sub was still out there, and he thought he could. Wherever it had temporarily gone, he thought it was back now. "Unless one person on each side is already part of a clandestine way to communicate."

"If you tell me that you and Markowitz used to have houses across the street from each other and used to communicate with flashlights when you were kids, I swear to God…"

"No. There's way too much of an age difference between us for us to have grown up with each other," Applebaum said. "But when he was a guest professor and I was a teacher's aide, we did work something out in order to try to catch a bunch of students we suspected of cheating. But it was by showing each other a certain number of blank pages from opposite sides of the room. Now all we would need to do is figure out how to do that with what we have available. Gorky, do you think you can get more of the lights back on? Both inside and out. I think we'll need everything at our disposal in order to interpret our old code."

"Yeah, I could do that," Gorky said, even though he was shaking his head.

"Why are you shaking your head?" Applebaum asked.

"Because only academics would go to so much trouble as creating a complex secret code to catch cheaters. You really didn't have anything better to do with your time?"

"Well, um, I guess we did, but what can I say? Sitting down and creating our own code was fun."

Gorky muttered something unbelieving under his breath but got to work. After about six or seven minutes, though, Gorky stopped and shook his head again. "I hate to break this to you, but I don't think we're going to be able to do anything of the sort. Not quickly at least. Maybe if you give me half an hour…"

"I don't know we have half an hour, but keep going just in case. I think… wait…"

From outside the fish, lights started flashing again, but these were definitely not from the anglerfish. They came and went too quickly, and they were in a pattern Applebaum thought he recognized. "Well I'll be damned," he said.

"What?" Gorky asked. "What is it?"

"It looks like I'm not the only one who thought of our little anti-cheater system," Applebaum said. "Markowitz interpreted it into a light pattern a little differently than I would have, but I definitely recognize it."

"You know, I've got to say," Gorky said, "it's a little freakish that you two know each other well enough to be able to think like each other that closely."

"What can I say?" Applebaum said. "We've seen a lot together. Now be quiet for a second. I need to concentrate on figuring out what he's trying to say."

He watched for several moments, his brain working as quickly as it could to rework the code. "I think he's saying they no longer have any contact with the ship? I feel like it's a little garbled, or maybe that's just because, you know, I'm trying to see it through the skin and ribcage of a fish."

"But does he say anything about coordinating our plan to get out?"

"It's not something I can ask without prompting if we don't have those lights ourselves."

"Fine, fine. Working on it."

Applebaum continued staring, hoping he wasn't missing some key bit of the flashing light code simply because he maybe didn't understand how Dr. Markowitz's brain worked quite as well as he thought he did. "I think he's trying to give us a specific time where we should try to get out. So that we're doing it at the same moment that they attack it from the outside."

"And what time exactly would that be?"

"Um, it might be a moment two minutes from now. Or maybe he's saying it will be two hours from now. Or possibly three. Minutes or hours. Or four? Damn it, maybe I'm not getting this as much as I thought I would."

"Well you better figure it out pretty quick," Gorky said, "because if we don't get it right, something tells me this isn't something we'll be able to try coordinating a second time. If they ram the fish and we don't get out, it's probably going to swim away. Or kill them. Or us. Or both."

"Just quiet, okay? I'm trying to concentrate. Is there a clock in here that's working?" He looked over at it. There was supposed to be a digital one, but that one was out. "You don't happen to have a watch, do you?"

Gorky undid his watch quickly and tossed it to Applebaum. "Okay," Applebaum finally said. "He was saying three minutes, I think. At exactly three fifty-nine p.m." He looked at Gorky and shrugged. "So I guess in two minutes and three seconds we're going to find out if we get to live."

CHAPTER ELEVEN

Markowitz carefully watched their target anglerfish, hoping that their message had actually reached someone inside alive enough to interpret and understand it. And if Applebaum was in some way incapacitated, all the complicated code work wouldn't help anyway. After an agonizing amount of time, though, something began happening from inside the fish. Something was moving, albeit slowly, and the fish started to rouse with the sensation of its prey, after hours of attempted digestion that should have killed it, regaining some will to live.

"Are you sure they understood what we were trying to tell them?" Morgan asked.

"No, I'm not. But I'm hoping that maybe Applebaum and myself think alike enough that it won't matter if he understood or not. He probably had a similar idea to me at the same time. I hope."

"Okay then," Morgan said with a noticeable nervous quaver in her voice as she looked at her watch. "Let's prepare to give this thing the mother of all belly jabs."

They backed the sub up slowly from their current position, always being acutely aware of the many other giant anglerfish in the area that could take the slightest movement as a sign to attack. Markowitz took note of the patterns they made around the sub and marveled when comparing this to what he knew about typical anglerfish. They were solitary creatures. This kind of grouping up and schooling was uncommon for them. He also didn't see any smaller males attached to larger females the way small anglerfish did, but there did seem to be some notable sexual dimorphism between some of them that indicated a difference between males and females. Again, all of it was completely new to science, and all of it needed further investigation. Of course, there would be no such investigation if everyone down here who witnessed it all ended up dead.

"You know, I would feel much better about this plan if it didn't just boil down to 'hey, let's headbutt the monster in the stomach,'" Morgan said.

"Let's be honest, though," Markowitz replied. "If we survived, that will be a hell of a sentence that we'll now be able to say in complete honesty."

"True. There is that. Here. Count us down." She took off her watch and handed it to Markowitz. He himself had stopped wearing watches years ago since his sea exploits had a tendency to ruin them, so he was glad that Morgan hadn't experienced that just yet.

"One minute, twenty seconds," he said.

"Are you sure this will be okay if he doesn't try to ram his way out of its throat at the same time as our attack?" she asked, then answered for herself. "Of course not. I'm rambling now. I should just shut up, stop jabbering. I should…" She realized what she was doing and cut herself off.

"And we're right about at one minute," Markowitz said. "We should… wait. Oh shit."

Morgan didn't have to ask what he was suddenly upset about. She could see the fish outside their window just as well as he could, and it was pretty obvious that the mishappen lump in its belly was suddenly trying to move.

"He got the code wrong for the time," Markowitz said. "Morgan, hit it! Quick!"

Even with Morgan moving as fast as she could, it was difficult for any human-made machine to do anything quickly in the deepest pressure regions of the ocean. Even as their sub was just starting to pick up a little speed, it was obvious that Applebaum's sub had already made its attempt. The anglerfish was clearly very agitated by the unprecedented movements going on within its stomach, and that seemed to be enough to temporarily distract it. But Markowitz was pretty sure that wouldn't be enough.

"Morgan, you need to…" He stopped himself as he realized he needed all her concentration on ramming the fish. Instead, he reached over in the cramped compartment and simultaneously flashed on all the sub's exterior lights at once. It would hardly have been considered much light on the surface, but down here, to a creature that only ever saw soft bioluminescence, it was absolutely blinding. The creature froze for just a second before it could swim off in alarm. Fortunately, that split second of hesitation was enough.

The nose of the sub hit the anglerfish at the back of its distended belly. The flesh of the giant fish's stomach softened the impact somewhat, but even with that in between they were still moving at close to the top speed right into another sub, one that was much sturdier than their own. Markowitz fell out of his seat with the impact, and although there were so many other sights and sounds happening at once he still thought he heard the sub groan under the force of the hit along with the water pressure. For the space of a heartbeat, he was convinced that they had compromised the integrity of their sub and the entire thing would crush in upon them before they had a chance to fully understand their fate, but that didn't happen.

What did happen was that their bump, along with another attempt to zoom out of the fish's stomach by the other sub, seemed to work. It was difficult to see completely from their vantage point, especially since they were still righting themselves after being thrown willy-nilly around the inside of their cockpit, but the anglerfish looked like it opened its massive lower jaw wide. Suddenly the hard material from inside the anglerfish's stomach was no longer pressed against them.

"Morgan, reorient us so we can better see the front of the fish," Markowitz said. "We need to make sure they got out before we try anything else."

"I'm trying, I'm trying," she said. "This thing isn't exactly handling like a fighter jet, you know. Not that I would know how a fighter jet handles, even though I would probably be pretty good at calculating how to do it. It's just that Tom Cruise makes it look so…"

"Not the time for a rambling rant, Morgan," Markowitz said.

"Right, right. Sorry."

At first it was hard to see anything at all other than a very large, very angry and confused anglerfish. It thrashed about, churning up the water, and once or twice its enormous tail hit the side of their sub, although not terribly hard. The fish obviously felt like it needed to fight something but wasn't quite sure what that something was or where it was being attacked from.

The other anglerfish, however, didn't seem to be having the same trouble. They must have been distant enough that the sudden flash of lights hadn't been enough to blind them, but it had been enough to alert them to a danger in their midst. A few were swimming away at speeds that Markowitz found astonishing and beautiful. Others were getting closer with the appearance of creatures ready for meals of their own.

"Keep the lights out now," Markowitz said. "It looks like…"

"Yep, I see it." She hit a number of switches, and even the interior lights went out. It suddenly made it very dark indeed inside their tiny vessel, but it provided the added benefit of them being better able to see anything casting light outside their submersible. And that included the other sub.

The first anglerfish, the one that had originally decided Applebaum's sub must be some kind of new delicacy to add to its diet, was keeping its distance now from the thing that had given it what was probably the worst case of indigestion it had ever experienced. The others, however, were getting closer and circling it in a decidedly aggressive manner.

"They're not actually going to try swallowing it again, are they?" Morgan asked. "They can't possibly still think of it as food after what happened to the other one."

"We have no way of knowing yet how intelligent they are," Markowitz said in response. "Maybe they are in fact capable of that level of problem solving. Or maybe they're just operating on pure instinct and thinking 'It's smaller than me, therefore it's food.'"

"If the sub gets swallowed again, I don't know if we'll be able to pull off another rescue," Morgan said. She looked at the various readouts in front of her and frowned, but she didn't elaborate on anything she might have seen in them. Markowitz almost asked if she saw anything worrying there, but he decided he'd rather not know, at least not yet. He only had room for one worry at a time, and for now that worry was going to be about Applebaum.

Most of the lights for the other sub were out, but as they watched, all exterior lights went out except for one. Strangely enough, it was a small light near the severed safety tether that had been ripped apart when the anglerfish had initially swallowed them. For several moments Markowitz didn't understand, but once he did a smile took over his whole face.

"Applebaum, you brilliant bastard. That's a spectacular idea," he said.

"What? What's he doing?" Morgan asked. Markowitz would have been surprised she didn't figure it out herself, except at no point did her attention seem to be going back to the other sub. She was intently working various controls and studying gauges.

"The initial pattern of lights on the sub when they first encountered the anglerfish must have come close to mimicking some kind of existing prey fish or animal down here," Markowitz said. "That's why it was so quick to attack. So if the sub can remind the fish of one thing, it can also remind them of something else if the pattern is different. Like, say, having a single light near a dangling piece over its front."

Morgan finally looked up from the controls to give him an appreciative smile. "Applebaum is trying to fool the giant anglerfish into thinking that their sub is one of the fish as well. That's really smart."

"And I think it's working," Markowitz said. "Most of the fish have stopped bothering it, although… hmmm. I'd be careful if I were him. If these main anglerfish are female, they might see the smaller size of the sub now as denoting a male, and they could try to mate with it." One or two of the fish that remained did indeed look to Markowitz like they could have amorous intentions for the sub, but once again he couldn't be sure. They had absolutely zero idea of the complexities of mating for this species.

"They're starting to go back up," Markowitz said triumphantly. "As long as we are careful with what exterior lights we keep on, we should be able to follow them and end this whole nightmare."

Morgan's response was very quiet and reserved. "Dr. Markowitz, I don't think we're going to be celebrating with them back on the boat."

Markowitz turned to her, and any mirth or joy that was in him went away as he saw the dire expression on her face. "What is it, Erin?"

Morgan pointed to one of the readouts on the control panel. "We must have taken some damage to the propulsion systems either when we hit the first anglerfish or when we got smacked by its tail. We're sinking."

Markowitz crowded into the small space next to her to take a look. "How fast?"

"Not fast at all, it looks like. Not enough that a sudden pressure differential will cause the sub to instantly implode. But the motors that would let us bring the sub back up are shot, I think. We probably won't even be able to go side to side or back and forth, let alone up or down by ourselves. They were never designed to take this kind of depth or strain. Which means…"

Markowitz finished for her in a melancholy yet resigned voice. "Which means every foot we drop is a foot we'll never regain. What goes down will never go back up."

CHAPTER TWELVE

Applebaum knew immediately that something had gone horribly wrong, but it took Gorky a little bit longer to see that they were the only sub rising in the water instead of falling. He was the one needing to keep control of the lights, after all, as well as making sure that they didn't ascend so fast as to trigger any of the anglerfish into aggression. He didn't seem to notice until he got an additional camera working, the one pointed down at where they had just been, and where the other sub still floated in the nothingness.

"Why aren't they following us?" Gorky asked. "We don't have time to dither around. All of us have to get back to the surface as quickly as we safely can."

"Stop the ascent," Applebaum said. "We can't go back up yet."

"Why not?" Gorky asked.

"Because I think Markowitz and whoever else may be in that sub are stuck. Or worse, I think maybe they might be sinking."

Although he was obviously reluctant about it, Gorky slowed their submersible to a stop. "We can't go back down any further. We're already risking too much just by staying still so close to these things."

"But we can't leave them behind, either," Applebaum said. "Especially not after they risked everything to save us."

"But how do you suggest we go back down through a school of sixty- or seventy-foot anglerfish?"

"Same way we came up out of them." Applebaum had come up with the idea of trying to mimic the lights of an anglerfish at the last possible moment, when he was sure another one of the fish was about to swallow them again. It seemed to have confused the fish to start with, but he had no idea if it would continue to do so.

"I don't know," Gorky said. "Some of those fish were still acting pretty aggressive to us. Maybe this species can be cannibals?"

"No, more likely they might be… you know what? Never mind."

"Oh no. You can't start a sentence like that and just not end it."

"Well, it's possible they were just being territorial," Applebaum said. "But I think it's more likely that they were looking to mate with us."

"You've got to be kidding me. You mean to tell me those fish were looking at us and getting horny?"

"I don't know that for certain. In fact, that would be a very different way of mating than what is seen in standard run of the mill anglerfish. But yes, they did show some signs that maybe they had amorous intentions for the sub."

"Jesus Christ," Gorky muttered under his breath, but despite his obvious reluctance and reservations, he started to send the sub down once more.

There were fewer of the monster anglerfish at the moment, only four that Applebaum could clearly see through the portholes and few cameras that were still working. But they had a lot of blind spots now, and these things had already shown that they could swim fast enough out of the blackness to catch them off guard. There could very well be many more just outside the limits of their vision.

Gorky also paid attention to the various dark places where something could be hiding just out of sight, and he gave a noticeable shudder. "You ever hear that story about the anglerfish in the alley?"

"I don't think anyone's going to be finding anglerfish in city alleys, Gorky."

"No, it wasn't a real anglerfish. This was from some podcast or something, I don't know. But the story goes that in a certain alley somewhere there's a guy just hanging around in the shadows and he'll ask anyone who passes by for a cigarette. But he's not really a guy, he's a fake guy, just dangling in the darkness like a puppet, and if anyone ever approaches him to give him the cigarette then something comes out of the darkness and that kind-hearted smoker disappears forever."

Applebaum turned away from the window to give Gorky an incredulous look. "For the love of God, why would you bring that story up now? As if I wasn't already terrified by the fact that we've already been swallowed whole by a monster anglerfish once today."

Gorky shrugged. "Hey man, maybe I just figured that if I had to have that nightmare fuel in my head right now, I didn't want to have it alone."

Applebaum shook his head. "Let's just concentrate. The other sub should be just below us. Let's carefully move over just a bit so we don't bump it. If it's already damaged, we don't want to do any more." He avoided talking about any damage their own sub had already suffered, especially since he thought he kept hearing groaning noises from the vehicle around them. Maybe those sounds were just his imagination. Or maybe they were the submersible starting to feel the effects of the crushing water pressure that it would have been able to ignore before it had been bathed for hours in digestive stomach acid. Applebaum had never had a problem with claustrophobia before, but he was beginning to feel it now.

"Alright, we're next to it," Gorky said. "But trying to stay next to it is going to be a problem, because it is sinking."

"How fast?"

"I don't know enough about that old sub's rating when it comes to depth, but I don't think they're in any immediate danger of getting so low that it could crush them. But we don't know how safe it is for us to go any deeper now, either, so I don't think we'll be able to stay beside them for too long."

"Move our sub around so I can get a better look at any damage through my window."

Gorky did as he was asked, and Applebaum spent a minute going over what he could see of the sub in the murky depths without turning on too many lights and attracting the anglerfish. He was the marine biologist here, not the engineer, and he wasn't terribly familiar with the older model sub. But he thought the propulsion systems looked shot. This was nothing that anyone would be able to fix from inside the vehicle. The right kind of submersible, like one used by big oil companies to perform maintenance on their deep-sea drilling operations, might have been able to do something to help them. But their own wouldn't have been able to do much even without their own damage to worry about.

"Dr. Applebaum?" Gorky asked after a protracted period of silence. "I know you don't want to hear this, especially after Markowitz or whoever in there risked their lives to save us, but I think we're not going to have any chance at all of helping them. I think we may have to let them go."

"This isn't *Frozen* and my name's not Elsa," Applebaum said. "I don't have to let anything go. There's got to be something we can do."

"Not unless we want to get swallowed again, probably not," Gorky said.

Those words started banging around in Applebaum's head like a bull in a china shop, knocking a lot of ideas loose and breaking preconceptions about what they should and should not do in this situation.

"Dr. Applebaum? You're being quiet for a long time with a funny look on your face. It's not making me feel particularly safe. You aren't actually thinking about us getting swallowed again, are you?"

"No, not at all. That would be ridiculous. *We* don't want to be the ones who get swallowed at all. We want to be the ones out here attracting attention and playing hard to get."

The other man stared at Applebaum blankly for several seconds, followed by several seconds of pure horror on his face before he spoke again. "Okay, so let me get this straight, because there's absolutely no way you're suggesting what I think you are," Gorky said.

"No, I probably am," Applebaum said back.

"You want us to try to convince one of those anglerfish out there, the ones big enough to actually swallow us, to instead swallow our friends drifting down to the bottom of the sea, and then after that you want to convince it that we are some kind of male anglerfish that it will want to mate with?"

"More or less, yeah."

"And, uh, what exactly happens if it chases us for mating and then catches us? What happens to the sub?"

"Probably nothing. It wouldn't be anything to worry about."

"Are you lying?"

"I don't know. Maybe. Who the hell even knows? We're literally learning everything humanity knows about this particular sub-species of anglerfish right now in real time. If it caught us, it could just rub up against us for a while. Or it could crack us wide open. The only thing I can guess is that the second option is slightly less likely."

"Slightly less," Gorky said in a moderately sarcastic tone. "I don't suppose you can give me any percentages on that, can you?"

"If I were Erin Morgan, I probably could," Applebaum said. "But right now, she's somewhere very high above us. Maybe you can ask her to calculate that for you if we make it back."

"How do you know she's not over there in the other sub with Markowitz?" Gorky asked.

"I'm hoping Dr. Markowitz wouldn't be reckless enough to go three or four hours deep into the ocean in a sub-optimal sub with only an intern to help him, but the more I think about it that does seem likely. And if that's the case, that's just one more life that depends on all of this working."

Gorky sighed but nodded. "I guess we need to start figuring this out then. What do we have to do first?"

CHAPTER THIRTEEN

"They're moving again," Markowitz said. Morgan had gone very quiet as she worked at the sub's controls, desperately trying any and all last-ditch efforts to keep their sub from falling to where it would never be found again. Her silence was very unnerving. While Markowitz didn't think it actually mattered at this point whether the other sub was moving, he just had to say it in order to fill the air with some kind of noise that wasn't the disturbing ticks and groans of their sub struggling against the pressure.

"What are they doing?" Morgan asked. Her voice was calm and quiet, like she herself didn't think the answer to her question actually mattered.

"It looks like they're trying to get one of their windows in a position where we can see it," Markowitz said. The other sub drifted around until he could see Applebaum's face looking at them from the other side. Despite his own impending death, it made him feel good to see his friend's face alive and relatively well.

There was a moment where Applebaum too returned that look of appreciation, but then it was blocked out as he pushed a piece of paper against the glass with a message written in ball-point pen.

Dr. M, you need one of the fish to swallow you.

Markowitz stared with dumbfounded wonder at the hastily scribbled sign in the other submersible's window. Was Applebaum seriously suggesting this? How on Earth (or even under its watery surface) did he think this would be at all helpful? He looked around their own cabin for anything that could be used for writing, but in their haste to prepare the second sub, journals or notebooks hadn't exactly been considered essential equipment.

"We need to find some way to write to them and communicate," Markowitz asked Morgan. "You don't happen to have anything, do you?"

"I left my purse topside," Morgan said. "I didn't think there would be a lot of need for it down here. It's sitting on a desk right next to the pad of paper where I told my family to get screwed." She paused and stared into space for a few seconds before adding, "Maybe we can fog up the window and draw in the condensation?"

"Good idea," Markowitz said. There was already condensation building on the inside of the windows, which was concerning enough because it meant something was probably wrong with the sub's internal environmental controls, and it was easy for him to add to it by breathing on the porthole. It was small, so he had to sum up all his feelings about this idea in as few letters as possible. After a few seconds of thinking about it, he drew in the condensation:

WTF?

"Not exactly eloquent, but to the point," Morgan said.

The other sub had to keep adjusting itself so that they could still see its porthole as their own sub continued to slowly drop deeper into the abyss. Markowitz could barely make out Applebaum scribbling furiously on a sheet of paper. It was hard to see any details of him, but he looked pretty haggard after having spent multiple hours inside a fish. That was part of what made what he was suggesting all the more unbelievable.

Just do it, the new sign said. *Trust us. We know what we're doing.*

"They don't really know what they're doing, do they?" Morgan asked.

"Nope. Almost certainly not," Markowitz said. "But we're going to do what they say anyway."

"How on earth is getting caught inside a giant anglerfish's stomach just like they were going to in any way help us?"

"Not a clue," Markowitz said. "But look at it this way. If we don't do what they say, we simply continue sinking deeper into the Marianas Trench until we go beyond this particular sub's pressure rating, and we get squished like a ball of tin foil. That's a definite. There's no way around it. But if whatever crazy thing they're going to try works, we might actually survive."

Morgan shook her head. "It's bad to be inside a giant fish, it's good to be inside a giant fish. You never know what's going to change from one moment to the next, I guess."

CHAPTER FOURTEEN

Applebaum had to write a few more hasty signs to make sure Markowitz understood that they needed to turn various lights on in order to make his sub look like some kind of prey fish, but it seemed like Markowitz had already figured that part out. They didn't have a lot of time, since they didn't know if the anglerfish would stop following something below a certain depth, but Applebaum at least made sure Markowitz understood not to do it until he and Gorky had reached something like a safe distance. They didn't want to accidentally get swallowed up right along with them, after all. He wasn't sure if two of the subs could fit into one of the anglerfish's distended bellies, but he didn't want to find out.

"I think we're a good distance away now," Gorky said.

"Not too far away, though," Applebaum said. "As soon as we get one of the fish to take the bait, literally, we're going to need to redirect its attention right away."

"I still need to point out for the record that there are an insane number of ways for this to go wrong, and no real guarantee that it's even possible for this plan to go right."

"Point duly noted and ignored," Applebaum said. "Make sure we're facing the right way to see the action. The last thing we need is for one of the fish to gobble them up while it's out of our sight and then hide among the others before we can figure out which one has them."

The other sub ended up in the view of their forward camera right as a number of lights on the outside of it lit up the depths. Applebaum shook his head.

"Too bright," he muttered. "A prey fish of any kind wouldn't have that much illumination."

Thankfully, yet again, Markowitz seemed to be on the same page without even needing to hear Applebaum voice his concerns. A couple of the lights went off, and while the effect wouldn't have fooled anything with higher brain functions, Applebaum thought it would be enough to convince one of the giant nearby predators that this might be a good thing to eat.

For half a minute there was nothing, and Applebaum started to wonder if maybe they had to find a way to goad one of the anglerfish in the direction of Markowitz's sub. When the moment finally came, however, it happened fast enough that Applebaum might have missed it if he were blinking. From out of the darkness a giant maw rushed forward and snapped shut completely over the sub. Applebaum almost cheered, except cheering his friend getting eaten didn't seem quite appropriate. Also, any thoughts of cheering went away when he saw this anglerfish's size.

"Uh, I think this one is bigger than any of the others," Gorky said. Applebaum had to agree. This one hadn't been with the school previously, or at the very least had been far enough away in the darkness that they hadn't been able to detect its presence. The anglerfish swam around a little in an agitated fashion, like it instantly regretted its meal, and as it turned to its side, Applebaum could see the faint glowing lights of the sub from inside the creature's translucent stomach.

"On to phase two," Applebaum said. "Get the same configuration of lights ready that we used earlier."

"And we're really sure we want to basically tell this thing 'Hey big boy, I'm horny and available?'"

"More likely it's 'big girl,' and yeah. Absolutely no way to back out now."

Gorky mumbled many unintelligible things under his breath as he did as he was told.

"Now get closer," Applebaum said, "but be ready to immediately start our ascent as fast as possible."

Again, the fish didn't seem terribly interested at first. In fact, some of the other anglerfish looked like they were taking a liking to them before their target did. Applebaum was ready to start worrying about that, but when the large one did finally start swimming towards them, all the others bolted into the deep. Apparently when the biggest fish wanted to get it on, none of the others were willing to mess with it.

"Okay, get moving," Applebaum said. "But don't get so far ahead of it that we lose it or cause it to lose interest."

"So we're just going to lead this thing up for miles and hope it stays interested the entire time, but doesn't get interested enough to crack us open?"

"Pretty much." As they started to move up, the anglerfish accelerated. "But, uh, maybe losing it isn't going to be an issue. I think this thing is going to be able to move faster than us most of the time."

As if in response, the anglerfish bumped into the sub hard. It wasn't exactly moving at ramming speed, but it was definitely aggressive in a way that didn't imply hunger. If it got close enough to hit or rub up against them too often, the already-damaged sub might end up suffering the same system failures that Markowitz's had.

"Yeah," Applebaum said. "Definitely go faster. Much faster."

"If we try to go up any faster, we might get decompression sickness," Gorky said.

"And if we don't go faster a giant monster anglerfish is about to try mating with us," Applebaum said. "And if it tries and fails that, it might decide we're better suited as food and we'll end up right back where we started along with our colleagues. I highly suggest carefully weighing those options and then going fucking faster!"

Gorky sighed. "Oh what the hell. Why not. Never gotten the bends before. This way I'll be able to say that I've done something that others haven't. It can't really be that bad, can it?"

Applebaum didn't say anything to that. It really could be that bad. It could be deadly, and even if it wasn't, the pain would be excruciating. But by this point, it wasn't like any of them had any other choices left.

"Alright, brace yourself," Gorky said. "Not only is this going to be a rough ride, but we are probably going to be feeling incredibly shitty very shortly." He toggled some switches, tapped some keys, and pulled some levers, only half of which Applebaum understood the purpose of. What he did understand was that the accelerated climb to the surface would put their bodies through far too much pressure change far too fast. The resulting buildup of nitrogen in their blood was going to be extremely painful.

But it would still be a better fate, hopefully, than many of the other things that could go wrong now, so Applebaum figured he would be able to deal with it.

"Is it still behind us?" Applebaum asked. Gorky didn't have to respond. Instead, there was another thud from outside as the fish ran into the sub again. "Okay. I'm assuming that's a yes."

It felt to Applebaum like they were in a high-speed chase, although whether that's what they were actually doing was entirely up to interpretation. Gorky estimated that they would be moving at the sub's top speed for over an hour with a monster anglerfish battering at them all the way, which might seem slow if it weren't for the fact that their trip down had been right around four hours long.

Gorky must have been thinking something along the same lines, because he said, "This is really going to suck, isn't it?"

"Oh yeah, definitely," Applebaum said. "But at least we're the ones on the outside of the fish's stomach this time. That has to count for something, right?"

There was another bang on the outside of the sub, this one harder than the last, and Gorky lost control of the direction they were going for just a moment before he could correct their course. "You know what? I'm really not that sure we have the better end of the deal."

*

"Those guys out there definitely have the better end of this deal," Morgan said. While it was really hard to see out of the translucent stomach at an angle that showed them anything, Markowitz had to agree. Applebaum and Gorky might be the ones getting chased by a giant anglerfish capable of swallowing them whole, but at least they had some control of the vehicle they were in. Markowitz and Morgan did not, and it was starting to show in the queasy look on Morgan's face. Motion sickness wasn't something Markowitz himself had usually been prone to throughout his life, but it was pretty much impossible not to feel sick when the fish that was more or less carrying them up from the depths of the ocean was darting back and forth at crazy speeds in an attempt to get with what it thought was a possible mate. At least the two of them had thought to strap back into their seats immediately after the terrifying moment where the anglerfish had swallowed them whole. Otherwise, they would have been pinballing all over the inside of the cabin.

"I think it might be working," Morgan said. It should have been something she said with hope or joy. Instead, it was immediately followed by her spewing her breakfast, which promptly spattered in a noxious mess all over the inside of the sub.

Despite his best heroic efforts, Markowitz soon followed suit.

"Oh God, this is worse than the Tilt-a-Whirl at the county fair when I was a kid," Morgan said. "And that so-called 'fun ride' is about as bad as a torture rack."

"Uh, if I pass out at some point," Markowitz said, "please make sure I don't choke to death on my own vomit."

"Can't make any promises like that, since I'll probably be the one to pass out first."

Markowitz felt a droplet hit him in the forehead from somewhere. "Gross. Our vomit is still falling on me from somewhere."

For a moment Morgan looked too tired and sick to react. Then a look of realization came onto her face and she jerked her head to look at the ceiling of the sub, which was actually kind of the sub's side right now thanks to the direction the fish around them was pointing. "Um, I don't think that was our upchuck, Dr. Markowitz."

Markowitz looked in the direction she was just in time for another droplet to get through and hit him in the cheek. She was right. That wasn't some rogue bodily fluid. There was a leak in the ceiling of the sub. He couldn't tell exactly where the water was coming in, given how dark it was inside here, but it was clear that it was coming from somewhere where water had no right to be.

"Oh shit. Not good," he said. "Not good at all."

"Wait, if there's a leak in the sub, shouldn't we just be imploding right away?" Morgan asked, then answered her own question. "No, because being in the stomach of the fish is protecting us from the worst of the sea's pressure, and the pressure is decreasing the higher the fish goes. But…"

Another droplet hit Markowitz in his nose. Unlike the first one, this droplet itched and stung where it hit. "Ow!" he said. "That wasn't water."

"That was the anglerfish's stomach acid," Morgan said.

Markowitz nodded, although with all the shaking it probably just looked like the same shaking that the rest of his body was doing. "The other sub was newer and strong enough to resist it. But ours isn't. The integrity of the hull is breaking down. There's no telling how much longer it will be before the acid breaks the hull wide open and we end up digesting in fish chyme."

"Actually, I think I might be able to calculate that," Morgan said. She tilted her head for a moment before a horrified, dejected look appeared on her face. "Oh."

"It's less time than it will take for us to reach the surface, isn't it?" Markowitz asked.

"Maybe. It could be close. We might still make it." Then she looked him directly in the eye. Her expression told him everything he needed to know even without her having to say the words. "But the odds are not in our favor."

Markowitz nodded again but didn't say anything. All he could make himself do as he was rattled back and forth in his seat was hope beyond hope that Applebaum would be able to pull this off.

*

"Gorky, I don't want to alarm you, but I think you have a right to know. I feel like something is changing in the anglerfish's behavior."

Applebaum had been noticing signs that something was different for the last twenty minutes, but at first he had dismissed them as him simply not knowing enough about this species. Now, however, it was getting increasingly difficult to deny that the danger was growing.

"You know, Doctor, I probably would have been perfectly fine living in ignorance. But now that you had to open your damn mouth, hit me with it. What's different and how bad is it?"

"It's getting more aggressive, I think."

"Funny. Here I've been thinking this entire time that it was already aggressive."

"Aggressive in a different way. Aggressive not in a 'I want to spawn your eggs' sort of way and instead aggressive in a 'I'm getting irrationally angry and would like to chew on your face' sort of way."

"So what I'm hearing is that you want me to go faster, no matter what terrible physical condition it might put us in when this is all over," Gorky said.

"Is it even possible for the sub to go faster?" Applebaum asked.

"Maybe. Maybe not. At our current rate, I'd say we're about twenty minutes away from the surface."

Applebaum nodded, but he wasn't sure whether or not they had that long. The problem was that he couldn't be completely positive what the enormous anglerfish was trying to accomplish anymore. Maybe it was still in a mating mood. Maybe it was annoyed that its potential mate kept retreating and was trying to show its displeasure. Maybe it had decided after all that they currently looked more like a snack than a mating partner. Or maybe the change of pressure as the fish doggedly pursued them was affecting the creature's brain functions.

The exact scientific reasoning could be speculated on later, if they survived. For now, the single most important thing was that the fish was keeping up enough to occasionally ram them, and each ram was a little harder than the last.

"Since you're disclosing things, Dr. Applebaum, maybe I should, too. We're experiencing more and more systems failures."

“Are these failures anything that I can do anything to fix or alleviate?” Applebaum asked.

“Not even close,” Gorky said.

“Then I really don’t want to know.”

“Also, I think I’m starting to not feel so good,” Gorky said.

“Me either,” Applebaum said.

Something scraped against the outside of the sub and filled the interior with an ear-splitting shriek. To Applebaum, it sounded like it could be a giant tooth scraping against the hull.

“Go faster anyway,” Applebaum said. “I don’t think that thing cares whether or not we get the bends.”

The color of the ocean outside their windows was getting lighter fast, and as they moved, they zipped past numerous small sea creatures of various shapes and sizes. None of them stuck around for long, though. If the sub didn’t spook them away, then the huge apex predator chasing them did.

“Five minutes max,” Gorky said. “Maybe quicker.”

The fish slammed into them. One of the instruments on Gorky’s panels emitted a terrible squawk of warning before all the camera screens went out.

“We’re flying blind now,” Gorky said. “Or we mostly are. There’re still a few instruments that are giving depth readings and they are…”

From outside the sub there was a sound that could have been them hitting something, or it could have been something exploding.

"Nope. Never mind. Depth readings are gone too."

We're not going to make it, Applebaum thought. He closed his eyes, convinced that death was going to come any moment now. All he had was Gorky's running commentary.

"Multiple leak warnings," Gorky muttered. He sounded like he was about to pass out. "Dr. Applebaum, I just want to say that it was a pleasure…"

Two things happened, one immediately after the other. The first was that they breached the surface with just enough velocity that the sub shot up ever so slightly into the air.

The second was that the anglerfish closed its mouth over the sub. But neither of the sub's occupants realized that. The pressure change was enough that both of them went unconscious.

CHAPTER FIFTEEN

Markowitz woke up to pain, feeling like his entire body had been torn apart and then badly put back together by Dr. Frankenstein when he was on a bender. He would have thought he was dead if it weren't for every nerve ending in his body feeling like it was on fire. In particular, all his joints were throbbing balls of magma. He was able to stay awake long enough to recognize what he was feeling as the bends, decompression sickness, before he passed out. He couldn't even stay conscious long enough to register where he was.

When he came to again, the pain had subsided somewhat, enough that he could stay awake long enough to take in his surroundings before he once more passed out. He was in a hospital room, which didn't make a lot of sense to his scrambled brain at first. Since when did the *Rachel Carson* have its own hospital room? Also, it seemed pretty large for a room, any room at all, that might be on the ship. He only had enough time to realize he wasn't on the boat at all, that he had to be in some real hospital on the mainland, before he passed out again.

The next time he woke, he realized he wasn't in the room alone. Not only was there another bed in the room that was occupied, but there was someone sitting in a chair on the room's other side. It took some effort for Markowitz to move his head enough to see that Applebaum was the other bed's occupant. He was awake, although when he saw Markowitz looking at him, he only had enough energy to slightly raise his hand in what might have been an attempt at a wave.

"Both of you are finally awake at the same time," the other person in the room said. Markowitz had trouble focusing on the man, but he clearly recognized the voice of the man that had been berating him over the radio. Despite how angry Captain Lewis had been at the time, there was none of that anger in his voice now. Instead, there was nothing but relief. "Although given your condition over the last few days, I don't expect that to happen for long. So I'll do my best to be brief before one or both of you passes out again."

The captain got up from his seat so he could stand between the two beds where they both could see him better. "We're at the closest hospital we could reach that was able to deal with both of your conditions."

Markowitz tried to ask what condition that might be, but he found that he didn't quite have enough energy to move his mouth.

"All four of you had decompression sickness after you came up, which is to be expected considering how fast you rose through the ocean. It's an absolute miracle that none of you died."

Applebaum tried to croak out a question, but it was unintelligible.

"I'm going to assume that's you asking about Gorky and Morgan. While you two are done with the main portion of your treatment, they're both still undergoing hyperbaric oxygen therapy." The captain looked directly at Markowitz and did something the doctor rarely saw him do. He smiled. "Which means you did it, you crazy bastard. You actually succeeded."

Markowitz finally realized that the captain was holding a manilla folder in his hand, but Lewis made no mention of it just yet. "Both of your submersibles are shot. They'll never go in the water again. And quite frankly, no one is quite sure how they managed not to implode, given the amount of damage the techs are seeing on them. You both got so incredibly lucky that it's pretty much incomprehensible."

Markowitz looked over at Applebaum, who looked like he could barely keep his eyes open. He had really done it. Both of them had, really. They had managed to do the impossible against an impossible group of foes.

"I think there's something else the two of you should know," the captain said. "Your two subs weren't the only things we pulled out of the water. You, uh, how should I put this? You brought a specimen with you."

The captain opened up the folder to show them both that it was filled with hard-copy photographs. Markowitz would have said that was a bit dramatic, that digital photos on an iPad would have been sufficient, but he hardly felt well enough for breathing right now, let alone talking.

Which was just as well, because the photos that Captain Lewis held in front of them were absolutely breathtaking, and some of the equipment next to Markowitz's bedside beeped at him in an annoyed fashion as he literally temporarily forgot to breathe. The thing that they had been able to pull out of the ocean completely lacked any menace or majesty that they had seen from it when they were in the deep darkness of the sea, but even in its damaged, collapsed form it was truly a sight to behold.

"What… what the hell even is that thing?" Applebaum croaked out in response to the photo. If Markowitz hadn't seen him actually say it, he probably wouldn't have been able to identify the voice through the raspiness. It was practically impossible to identify, yet Markowitz understood what he was seeing all the same. There was a famous photo in marine biology of a *psychrolutes marcidus*, a deep-sea creature that, when it was photographed for the first time after being hauled from its proper place in the sea and plopped unceremoniously on dry land, looked very ugly and sad, which had led to its popular name: the blobfish. It wasn't until later that people realized that the fish didn't really look anything like that in its natural environment. At home deep in the ocean, the seemingly pathetic looking creature actually appeared rather fearsome.

And something very similar had happened here.

The giant anglerfish had been terrifying in the deep dark reaches of the ocean, a monster that would likely haunt the dreams of all four people who had been down there to see it. But it was easy to see why Applebaum couldn't recognize the thing anymore. After all, nothing was supposed to go from the hard pressure of the Marianas Trench to the surface. Markowitz and Applebaum were currently learning that the hard way, just as Morgan and Gorky would be in another room. But they had had the protective environments of the subs to withstand the rapid environmental change. The anglerfish had not.

The picture showed something that could indeed have been a cousin of the blobfish, provided that blobfish had mated with Godzilla and the resulting offspring had gotten caught in a garbage compactor. It was spread out on the deck of the *Rachel Carson*, or at least as spread out as the huge thing could be when it was in fact just about as long as the ship was wide. It must have realized something terrible was happening to it as it had quickly risen up from the depths after its mate or prey or whatever it had decided Applebaum's submersible was, yet it had still been compelled to continue the chase. That was behavior worth studying, presuming Markowitz ever felt able to get out of this bed again. For whatever reason, it had followed the entire way, and the squishy remains on the deck were all that was left.

Other pictures in the folder showed specific details, including the massive slit that had been cut in its belly to get their subs out of it. Other pictures showed structures that were only barely recognizable as eyes, teeth, and one that might have been that glowing antenna. The mushy looking bulb of it that lay on the deck would certainly never glow again.

All of that was sad to Markowitz in a way, like watching a spectacular and mighty opponent that had once inspired awe but now looked sad, ugly, and even a little pathetic. But that feeling passed for him quickly. There was relief that the beast was dead and wouldn't be swallowing anyone ever again, that was true, but that still wasn't the most prominent feeling Markowitz suddenly experienced.

It was glee. Not that the creature was dead, but that they now had a complete, if mushy, specimen of a giant sea creature that twenty-four hours earlier had been completely unknown to science. And, once he no longer felt like death completely warmed over, he and his greatest student would be the first ones who would get to study it. Erin Morgan would likely be there too right by their side, making her own observations and calculations along the way.

Gorky would probably sit that part out, though. Markowitz couldn't picture that man ever wanting to have anything to do with this thing ever again.

As all these thoughts went through his mind, Applebaum himself seemed to finally realize what he was seeing. "Oh," he said weakly. "Oh shit. Oh damn, this is going to be amazing."

The captain sighed. "I figured you two would actually be freakish enough to be happy that the thing that tried to kill you both was still with us. I've got to tell you, trying to fish that thing out of the water, no pun intended, while still keeping it mostly intact was a task and a half."

"Why would you do that?" Markowitz asked. "Preserving a specimen is hardly part of your job."

"And believe me, since the weather was getting rougher the whole time, I was very tempted to just peel off a few parts and then leave the rest to sink back into the sea."

"Then what made you decide differently?" Applebaum asked.

To Markowitz's shock, Captain Lewis actually smiled at them both. "You two managed to do some things today that probably should have been impossible. If you could do that, I figured I could get one fish out of the sea to give you both as a gift of appreciation that you're alive."

The captain put all of the photos back in order in the folder and closed it. "I'm going to leave you two alone for a while. There's going to be a lot to do later. Paperwork, reports, and of course the news media. They're already having a field day with this story. I'm sure you'll both want to make statements, and you'll probably want to see Gorky and Morgan at some point. But all of that is going to have to happen later. You both have a long period of recovery ahead of you."

Markowitz wanted to say thank you, but he could already feel his energy ebbing enough to send him back towards sleep. Instead, he just nodded at the captain as the man left.

Before he lost consciousness again, Markowitz moved his head one last time to look at Applebaum. Applebaum saw it, and the faintest of smiles came to his lips.

"Thank you for saving me," Applebaum whispered.

"You're welcome," Markowitz said. "And thank you for doing the same for me."

He never did find out if Applebaum said he was welcome back. Instead, Dr. Markowitz drifted off to sleep, on his way to recovery, along with dreams of monsters from the deep and scientific discoveries beyond imagination.

The End

SEVEREDPRESS

@severedpress
/severedpress

Check out other great

Sea Monster Novels!

Robert J. Stava

NEPTUNES RECKONING

At the easternmost end of Long Island lies a seaside town known as Montauk. Ground Zero on the Eastern seaboard for all manner of conspiracy theories involving it's hidden Cold War military base, rumors of time-travel experiments and alien visitors... For renowned Naval historian William Vanek it's the where his grandfather's ship went down on a Top Secret mission during WWII code-named "Neptune's Reckoning". Together with Marine Biologist Daniel Cheung and disgraced French underwater explorer Arnaud Navarre, he's about to discover the truth behind the urban legends: a nightmare from beyond space and time that has been reawakened by global warming and toxic dumping, a nightmare the government tried to keep submerged. Neptune's Reckoning. Terror knows no depth

Bestselling collection

DEAD BAIT

A husband hell-bent on revenge hunts a Wereshark... A Russian mail order bride with a fishy secret... Crabs with a collective consciousness... A vampire who transforms into a Candiru... Zombie piranha...Bait that will have you crawling out of your skin and more. Drawing on horror, humor with a helping of dark fantasy and a touch of deviance, these 19 contemporary stories pay homage to the monsters that lurk in the murky waters of our imaginations. If you thought it was safe to go back in the water... Think Again!

Printed in Dunstable, United Kingdom

80879133R00080